A THOUGHT WITHOUT COLLISION

ADRIAN DUNCAN

Tuskar Rock Press

First published in Great Britain in 2026 by
Tuskar Rock Press,
an imprint of Profile Books Ltd
29 Cloth Fair
London
EC1A 7JQ

www.serpentstail.com

1 3 5 7 9 10 8 6 4 2

Typeset by seagulls.net

Printed and bound in Great Britain by
CPI Group (UK) Ltd, Croydon, CR0 4YY

A CIP catalogue record for this book is available from the British Library.

Our product safety representative in the EU is BGC Sustainability & Compliance, 7 avenue du Général Leclerc, Paris, 75014, France
https://baldwinglobalconsulting.com

ISBN 978 1 80522 197 5
eISBN 978 1 80522 198 2

MIX
Paper | Supporting responsible forestry
FSC® C013604

Praise for Adrian Duncan

'Adrian Duncan's account of a mathematical prodigy and the characters who shape her life is for me his best work yet. The dual timelines build into a compelling enquiry into how we perceive and affect the world that we pass through. It's very moving, very funny, and it will make your brain dance' Jo Lloyd

'Adrian Duncan writes with emotional accuracy and what seems like effortless precision about work and exile, about buildings and cities. To his narratives, he brings a mixture of the exact and the visionary. To his characters, he brings a rawness of feeling combined with an urgent need for them to make sense of the world ... he is an original voice, a writer who has come to recreate the world on his own terms' Colm Tóibín

'A deliberative and delicate reading experience, revelatory in the truest sense of that word' *Guardian*

'This captivating fiction is a moving tribute to making, in all its forms' *Irish Times*

'There are shades of Beckett [and] W. G. Sebald … Conjures a deep and strange sense of stillness that hints at a discomfiting truth: this is a material world and we are merely passing through it' *The Times*

'Many have seen the tendency among Irish writers … towards experimentation as originating in this sense of foundational linguistic dispossession … Duncan proves himself to be one of the most subtle explorers of this condition writing today' *Literary Review*

'The kind of work that makes you remember why you read' *Sunday Business Post*

ALSO BY ADRIAN DUNCAN

The Gorgeous Inertia of the Earth
The Geometer Lobachevsky
Midfield Dynamo (short stories)
A Sabbatical in Leipzig
Love Notes from a German Building Site

Little Republics: The Story of Bungalow Bliss
(non-fiction)

To my sister Sallyanne

A judgement for me is not the mere grasping of a thought, but the admission of its truth.

Gottlob Frege, from *On Sense and Reference*

0.

Imagine you are sitting at a piano, with the forefinger of each hand hovering above the keys to the left and right of middle C.

Imagine first playing the right-hand key; then, after the note runs out, the left. Then you lift and place your right forefinger on the next note to the right and play that key once, and then, with the forefinger of your left hand, you play the second key to the left of middle C.

Imagine playing like this: one note, then the other, one, the other, one, the other, one, the other ... your arms moving all the way out towards the ends of the keyboard.

The structure of what follows is similar:

Parts '1.' are the right-hand notes, ascending.

Parts '2.' are the left-hand notes, descending.

I.

A young girl, on the morning of her sixth birthday, stands in a shaft of light at the rear door of a two-storey farmhouse, three fields east of a broad lake lined with deciduous trees all in early bloom. Behind this farmhouse rises a forest of evergreens and beyond roll hectares of pasture that transform into patches of gleaming turloughs, then undulating and open bog, a crescent-shaped township to house bog workers, then fallow fields, a man-made lake, a limestone quarry.

This girl, who has bobbed black hair, is being called to by her mother: 'Catherine, come back here at once!' she cries.

Catherine's mother, her father and her father's elderly mother stand in a row, and before them, in the middle of a pitted yard, a photographer bends to his camera and tripod, the blackening-out cloth draped over his head, neck and shoulders. Around his feet a gaggle of brown hens coo and cluck, while overhead flies a loosening V of calling geese.

The staring blue eye of the photographer, in the tent-darkness under his cloth, advances on the glass plate, which splays onto his retina the ghostly sight of an upside-down two-storey gable, three formally dressed upside-down adults, two looking outward, one, the mother, turned back towards the rear door of the house, beckoning Catherine to them.

Catherine hesitates, her dark upside-down eyes roving between the photographer and this – to her – unnatural arrangement of adults, standing in a line and facing the morning sun.

She wonders what strange spell this man and his contraption have over her parents and grandparent.

Her father leans forward and says through gritted teeth, 'Elizabeth, please put some order on that child!'

Catherine steps towards her mother, Elizabeth, dropping a ball of red string as she goes.

The photographer takes hold of the shutter and enters into those last few upside-down moments of composition before the chaos of the world disappears, then reappears, but now with an impression of it congealing onto a square plate of metal, coated over in sharp-smelling chemicals.

2.

A man in his mid-fifties rises from his bed and closes over his window that had been rapping gently against its frame.

Bleary-eyed, he sits at a wooden table in the middle of the attic room with roof joists canting overhead, and he rubs his neck. Pushing aside a notebook filled with sketches of simple arrangements of primary shapes, he opens out instead a lined notebook and carefully inscribes the words: *When I call you, come in through the door.*

As he writes, he realises that, were he to say these words aloud to someone, it would be assumed between him and his out-of-sight interlocutor that not only would there be a door to open, but also a doorway and a set of hinges from which the door cantilevers, and these hinges would be connected to a door frame in a wall, the wall to a floor and the floor to a shelter, the shelter to a stable rectangle of ground, and the person outside the door would be there out of a miraculous cosmic chance similar in probability to the person who called.

He looks to the door of his room and repeats aloud the sentence he has just written into his notebook.

Then, writing out and circling the word *hinges*, he rises awkwardly, squeaking his chair back across the shining floor, and steps to a wooden table in the corner of the room upon which sit two models of this house – one complete, the other he partially burned down on a blowy afternoon last week to see how his own house might burn were it to be set alight. He makes a note beside a line on a sheet of paper showing the ground-floor plan of this house, and then, with floorboards creaking underfoot, he makes for the bedroom window, opens it out fully once more, looks across the bright strand and the North Sea shifting in the distance, and then he reclines in increments back onto his bed.

His curly hair shivers about in the passing breeze, while the waves in the distance crash into the slow sorts of rhythms he recognises now as those belonging to the moments when the late morning of a breezy day, around here, turns into midday.

This man is more unwell than he believes and will perish in one month and eleven days.

I.

Before the photographer's shutter closes over, little Catherine suddenly pulls away from her mother and runs back to the kitchen door.

The photographer, exasperated at this ruined plate, looks up from his camera. The blackening-out cloth he now holds unwittingly at his chest in the style of a lord grasping a napkin at a celebratory meal. But because Catherine's father is well respected in this area, the lanky, blond photographer dare not express his exasperation. He imagines this photograph, if it were ever printed, as consisting of three handsome and well-dressed adults smiling in the sun, while to their left would curve a hip-high smear of movement from the mother to the rear door of the house, and within that smear might appear an errant leg, a finger, a child's staring eye.

Catherine points in through the door, while her mother, Elizabeth, a slim and dark-haired Englishwoman in her early thirties, takes Catherine's arm and pulls her back into the yard. In an armchair in the kitchen, the girl's uncle snoozes. Behind him, the yellow sunlight reaches across the stone floor and into this sunlight then appears the strange four-legged and two-headed shadow-creature of this young girl being tugged at by her mother. The uncle is blissfully unaware that Catherine feels strongly that he ought to be part of this family event. The uncle, though, is a conniving sort and he wants no part in the photograph because – as he stated earlier in the morning at the bustling kitchen table, a spoon laden with shining raspberry preserve at his lips – he doesn't want any evidence of his being here. 'For reasons of tax, Moore,' he concluded, to his younger brother and the owner of this farm. For reasons of tax there can be no evidence of him in this country for equal to or more than six months per calendar year.

Catherine is returned to the line of adults standing stiffly in the farmyard. She places her arms in an X before her and frowns.

'Leave Uncle Gilbert be, child,' hisses Moore.

The photographer then takes hold of the shutter, raises his left arm, and from his mouth come the words: 'While we have the good light, can we all hold still for a few seconds there, in five, four, three, two …'

2.

The curly-haired man in his mid-fifties, in a rare bout of vigour, decides to take a walk along the beach that lies a short distance east of his house.

The strand is empty except for a young family picnicking far behind him in a small inlet, sheltered by white and grey crags. He empties and fills his lungs with sea air as he walks, his broad cotton trousers flapping in the breeze, while he carries a leather sandal in each hand.

As he goes, he remembers an old friend and colleague, Peters, with whom he once, as a young man, designed a large box kite. He recalls the first time, on a blustery afternoon in a lake bay some miles south of Bolzano and near the technical university where he and his friend studied, when the kite left his hands and took to the skies. He remembers how for several magical minutes they watched their white kite float over and back in the Dolomitian sky and how the string in Peters' hands tautened and released as the kite translated its buffeting and soaring to the ground. He analysed for some time the swerving flight of this box kite, high in the cloudy firmament, and then imagined, as the kite went higher still, the improvements he would make to the aeronautics of its shape.

The kite crashed down moments later, and with that an erosion began into the young man's interest in aeronautical engineering.

He realises, as he comes to a halt along this beach, that, had this kite not plummeted groundward between the available currents of ripening air that day, many years ago, and if the kite had not split along two of its main struts, then perhaps today he would still be working in aeronautics and solving interesting problems in laminar and turbulent airflow. Some part of him always knew that he would never master the problem of turbulence, but perhaps, he thinks, as he straightens from his knees, his shortening breath now almost caught, he could have at least helped advance the discipline of aeronautics into the complexities of turbulence with a type of cautious creativity more to his liking.

With the tangy scent of seaweed wafting towards him on a breeze, he turns a good half mile short of the end of the strand and makes his way back towards the western corner, where, behind hillocks and two leaning trees, lies his modest self-built house. In the distance, the picnicking family have since gathered up their belongings in a wicker basket and are trudging towards the dunes.

The curly-haired man in his mid-fifties sits at his kitchen table.

Outside, the breeze strengthens, sending creaks down into the structure. His face is pale and the darkness around his blue eyes grows darker as he sits silently at the table, looking at a tremor in his hands. He goes to his room upstairs, where, almost as if to pause this tremor, he writes (in German) the words:

> *What is a train track when a train is not passing or has never passed over it? Is a train track's road-worthiness not required for one to designate it so? What if the gauge of this track fits no extant train? What is a train track when it is lifted and bent and broken, with an upturned engine and carriages hundreds-of-yards beyond, lying in smouldering fires along the siding? Is it not then merely a tool used to lift trains irrevocably beyond their centres of gravity? What is it when the track is out of use and tufts of grass grow up from between what is left of the crumbling timber sleepers and no train has passed over its rails in years?*

He looks at his watch and returns downstairs, where he sets a large dark pot on his range to boil. He then lifts a skillet from the wall and begins to heat it up. He takes butter from his tiny pantry and carves a half-inch cube from it. Then he takes a delph pot from a cupboard and from it lifts two eggs, with which to prepare an omelette.

That night, he sleeps for fifteen hours, and wakes to knocking downstairs.

When he looks at his watch, he can scarcely believe his eyes. He begins to wonder what day it is. He lumbers downstairs to his front porch to admit the knocker, a doctor who has recently received a report, from the city's main hospital, on this man's bloods.

'Dr Bain, welcome,' he says, while stepping aside and offering his visitor entry.

'Thank you, Dr Alois,' replies Dr Bain in his thick Scottish accent, 'and how are you feeling today, sir?'

I.

Young Catherine hunkers in the yard looking on at two hens pecking the ground.

One soon shows itself to be more dominant than the other and is eating most of the seeds. Catherine wonders if she should intervene and help this weaker hen by shooing the larger one away.

Above her at a first-floor bedroom window, her grandmother appears. She gazes out across the land and the lake. She's no longer on speaking terms with her eldest son, Gilbert, and has now come to greatly dislike his visits, which upset the equilibrium in the house – the otherwise unspoken but peaceful hierarchies. She often wonders why this son of hers cannot simply pay some tax in one country or another.

Downstairs in the sitting room, plump little Gilbert stands, smoking a pipe, as Moore, alongside him, sits back into an armchair. Their pale eyes scan the same sparkling lake below while they both listen to the BBC presenter on the wireless give staid updates on how the Dow Jones and the London Stock Exchange are performing at midday. Gilbert owns shares in reputable companies in the UK and is so obsessively careful with his money that he chooses to live for five months and twenty-nine days every year on the island of Guernsey in the English Channel. He spends two, for him, arduous days each year travelling over and back between the Irish midlands and Guernsey, in a lucrative no-man's land of gentle seas, stinking harbours, cramped trains. Both men grunt in satisfaction at the numbers being announced from the wireless perched up on the mantelpiece. Moore absent-mindedly runs the palm of his hand over his pate, touching the tips of the last few hairs wavering there like wisps of smoke across an exhausted terrain. These two well-educated brothers dabble often in monetarism, a new science of trading future values of foreign currency. Once the British pound was liberated from the gold standard, they corresponded daily with each other, speculating as to what would fill the lack of stability, what now, as Gilbert put it, 'would tether this money to the ores of the earth'. Last year, they each made several thousand pounds. Gilbert cashed out of this monetarism and has advised Moore to do the same – 'A bird in the hand, dear brother, a bird in the hand!' They listen as the wireless crackles over numbers being called out by an otherwise steady Scottish voice – the sort of voice one might hear on the same radio station late at night, on a shipping forecast, relaying wind speeds off some distant northern coastline: *twenty-seven miles, a thousand and seventeen, east south-east five, falling slowly …*

Catherine runs down the steps at the bay window before them, where she then plays in the pink flowers beneath. She's making to plod into the vegetable patch when her father, returning his watch to his pocket, leans forward and raps the window. She looks over her shoulder; then, smiling widely, she gathers up the loose folds of her red frock in one hand and chases back towards the yard.

Upstairs, the mother of the two men downstairs can hear Elizabeth crying in the main bedroom at the end of the corridor. Elizabeth tries to stifle these cries because she knows that sobs of this kind can be heard right through the house. She has heard her mother-in-law keen anciently on many nights, to which Moore merely raises the volume of the wireless in the kitchen or dining room and moves to another room.

Elizabeth has received upsetting news from London about her youngest sister, who is to marry a man Elizabeth knows to be pernicious, violent. She herself once went out with this man, when she was much younger, until, late one night, while they were walking back towards her parents' house in Hoxton, he forced himself upon her and struck her when she wouldn't relent to his desires. She said nothing of it at the time, one didn't, but from then on out she decided to avoid handsome young men of that swaggering kind and plumped instead for this gentle if stolid Irishman she met through a friend who worked in the bank in which he, Moore Carolan, was also then employed. Elizabeth, taking her red cardigan from her blotchy face, looks out at the same lake her husband, a floor below, gazes over and, stemming tears from her large blue eyes, resolves to travel back to London to see if she can dissuade her naive younger sister from marrying this no-good. She pushes her fine dark hair back from her face.

Downstairs, Moore, who was alerted to this troubling news this morning, mere minutes before the photographer arrived, is of the same mind, but he cannot let Elizabeth travel until she has accepted the latest wording of his will – a wording that she struggles to accept, especially around percentages of wealth and land due, in the absence of a son, to 'the next of kin'.

Catherine climbs the half-turn staircase up to the first floor, now flooded in afternoon light. She passes the room in which her grandmother, having stepped back from the window, now dozes, and she continues on to her mother's bedroom, where she stands at the door and knocks. Elizabeth, drying her eyes with a knuckle, bids her daughter to 'Please, enter.'

At this moment, on the opposite side of the county, the lanky blond photographer swerves along a hedge-lined country road, en route to the nearest town of B_, where he will unload his equipment and begin developing in the tiny darkroom in his lodgings the photographs of this Carolan family and their restless girl. His second-hand Model T – recently lifted off a railway wagon that had arrived up from Cork city – rattles along these inchoate and at times bumpy roads.

In the fields to his right, a half-built pylon bends crookedly to the ground, with steel elements in a ring of loose lines at its base. It is the first of many being erected to hold aloft a high-voltage cable that will run from the planned hydroelectric power station in Shannon to Birr, in the southern midlands, and from there, it is envisioned, this cable will run east and on to Dublin. The photographer's grey-blue eyes return to the road. He is in love with a woman in the smaller district to the west of the town of B_. When he speeds through the countryside like this, his mind often fills with images of this woman in various states of undress. He imagines her often on an ornate chaise longue, gazing at him while lifting the hem of her white silk nightdress above her knee. There are moments in his day that he would like to push this hem much further up her thigh, and these moments then translate into a hardening in his trousers and the words in his mind that say, *Christ, I'd give my eye teeth for five minutes with that Clare Dargan*. He imagines his seed speeding towards her and spilling onto her belly. He wonders, does his pornographic framing of her thusly in his mind stem from him spending so much time looking down a lens and cauterising away so much of what is human in the world – his making of subjects into objects? Clare Dargan is a butcher's daughter, recently motherless, and is in love with a schoolteacher, a callow young man called Francis who is not from this part of the country. His family owns a two-roomed cottage on a small parcel of land at the end of a frothing peninsula on the most western tip of the Kingdom of Kerry. It is a bleak place, which Francis now rarely visits. The squalor and hardships became unbearable to him a term or two after he'd received a scholarship to study Latin and English in Dublin. Francis, known locally as 'Master Francis', is newly graduated from training college in Dublin, and has been posted to this small country school for the last three terms. His most recent intake includes six-year-old Catherine Carolan, whom the photographer photographed not an hour ago. Master Francis is what is referred to as a *Gaeilgeoir*, a fluent Irish speaker, and this, in the eyes of the photographer, makes him a maudlin traditionalist from a disappearing era.

The photographer's long fingers grasp the steering wheel as he accelerates down the hill towards B_. He drives with the aim of soon visiting and perhaps flirting with this Clare Dargan, in the hope of making her his.

At this same moment, young Catherine climbs onto the seat at the end of her mother's bed. Elizabeth, now with her red cardigan draped over her shoulders, shifts towards her bedside table to compose a letter to her sister in which she implores her not to marry this man. She says she will explain fully when she sees her in the coming weeks.

Catherine, listless at her mother's inattention, slips back out of the room and makes her way down the corridor and through the light slanting from the tall windows. In the other bedroom, Catherine finds her grandmother slumped awkwardly on the bed, her face a sunken moon poking out from an inert landscape of black shawls. Catherine advances on her and sticks a little finger up into her grandmother's left nostril. She starts awake, but Catherine, laughing, runs from the bedroom, down the stairs, along the corridor and into the sitting room, where her uncle and father still smoke as they listen to a movement of classical music drifting gaily from the wireless. Her father asks her to leave, to take up a picture book 'or some such' in the kitchen and 'put a stick on the fire, like a good girl'.

The grandmother, upstairs, smacks her lips, rubs her nose, looks around and then closes her small dark eyes once more. She would dearly like to return to the dreamlike thoughts she was falling into in those moments before her nose had been so wantonly fingered by her granddaughter ... shimmering thoughts of her now long-deceased husband on the first day she saw him, in her childhood town, far out on the Allihies peninsula. Her then husband-to-be wears a pale short-sleeved shirt, wind-bitten from summers of work at sea. He steps from his fishing boat bobbing at the harbour wall, and she admires his dark locks and his broad shoulders, the confidence of his footing on his small tilting boat and how he so easily manipulates his length of heavy rope. She cannot swim and fears the day he might invite her for a dip in the cove way off to the right of the harbour, shielded from view of the town by a grouping of crags into which now beat the sea waves. She has never been with a man before, but she knows what goes on often over there in that private and godless cove, that place of admiration and confusion. Her heart lifts as her husband-to-be looks up from the harbour wall, takes her in awhile, smiles and waves.

The grandmother opens her eyes to the sound of her granddaughter, Catherine, screaming downstairs. Footsteps funnel in thumps along the upper and lower corridors and towards the kitchen below. The grandmother, hurtled from her serene tidal thoughts, rises and carefully makes her way down the stairwell to the kitchen, where Elizabeth holds a tearful Catherine as Moore inspects the child's arm.

‘Surface burn,’ he concludes, and bends to kiss her brow. He touches her cheek; then, from the pantry, he retrieves the butter dish, while Elizabeth takes her daughter’s head in her arms, strokes her dark hair, pushes the tears from her puce cheeks and begins to coo.

‘This girl needs a brother, Moore,’ says his mother, standing at the jamb of the door.

Elizabeth looks up at her mother-in-law – on the cusp of saying something – then, she looks to her husband, who looks at her in that straightforward and at times expressionless way of his, almost allowing her to intuit what she wishes from his face. Today, she reads a plea for quiet.

Moore then bends to Catherine and blows cool air from his lips while rubbing a dollop of butter onto her limp forearm as it all comes up in a glowing red.

A lone clucking hen stalks in through the door of the kitchen. Moore makes to shoo it away; the hen disappears with a dust-lifting clatter.

2.

In his kitchen, Dr Alois sets two places, one at either end of a broad table he made some years back with leftover wall planks he then planed to shining smoothness.

In the centre of the table, a candle flickers alongside a silver vase filled with recently picked white flowers. In a pot on his stove, two chicken legs cook in their own fat. Alois killed the last of his hens yesterday evening in his backyard, wringing its neck before bringing his knife down upon its gullet. He'd not done this in some time, in fact he could not recall the last, and from his lips, as the hen's body writhed – blood spurting from its neck – came the whispered word, 'Damnation.'

He reclines on his couch and immediately falls asleep.

The sunlight slanting across the jugs of water on his windowsill comes and goes. The clock above the dresser ticks, while on his wrist the minute hand of his watch falls towards the six, bisecting the word LIECHTENSTEIN, printed in small gothic capitals across the face a few millimetres below the turning point of the three splayed hands. This watch was gifted to him by his mother on his first day at the university in Bolzano. It had been gifted to her by her father on the morning she left her home in Vaduz for her new life of marriage to a Manfred Alois, the owner of a vineyard on the southern slopes of Kaltern in South Tyrol. Outside, the wind rises, recedes and rises once again, into a musical series of ascending gusts. A fly soars from one windowpane to another, to the door, then back to the first window. The chicken legs in the pot begin to brown. Dr Alois breathes gently, his right hand resting on his sternum, the index finger rising every now and then as if lifted by an invisible string. The minute hand on his watch passes nine and then climbs onto ten, and, at this, Dr Alois stirs. He opens his eyes, blinks, rubs his mouth, and, as is his wont in these moments of waking, he suddenly rises and searches his pockets for a pencil, then he climbs the stairs to his room, where he sits at his desk to write what was in his mind in that gorgeous, fertile moment between sleeping and waking.

He takes his seat, but then falters, as if what was in his mind is too difficult to put into words, or the words he chooses fail to take sufficient hold of the undersides of what was in his mind, tugging it landward. He opens out his other, unlined notebook instead and draws onto the recto page a red cone, and behind it a green circle. He carefully colours these two shapes with pencils. Studying this arrangement awhile, he then redraws it on the verso page, but now with a red circle in front of a green cone, its centre coinciding with the tip. He looks at this awhile too, in an impotent attempt to eke meaning from the differences in these arrangements.

Behind him, through the window of his bedroom appears, in the distance, between the wavering dunes and the row of newly built beach bungalows, his guest – a handsome woman in her mid-thirties. The wind ruffles her dark hair as she carries a canvas bag and a wicker basket filled with foodstuffs, changes of clothing, her notebooks, her books and a four-day-old letter from Alois asking her urgently to visit.

Dr Alois, gazing on at his notebook, realises, as he retouches an incompletion in these drawings of circles and cones, that his capacity for bringing his sleeping life into his waking one is waning. He writes, with a degree of disappointment, at the base of the green cone, the word *Windmill*.

1.

From the kitchen of the farmhouse, Catherine, blindfolded and smiling, is being led by her parents to the dining room, where, beside the unlit fireplace, awaits a red tricycle. In the sitting room, her grandmother crochets a navy-and-green scarf, while Gilbert sits opposite reading from the business pages of *The Manchester Guardian*, a newspaper he irons each morning in his garters and underpants. Gilbert notices Catherine, Elizabeth and Moore creeping past, smiles, puts his rustling paper aside, and rises to join them in the dining room, now cold from the unlit fire. The windows to the left and right of the fireplace display fallow fields shivering down to rows of hedges leading towards the lake. The sun has come back out again, after an hour and more of rain, and the lowing cattle and the trees and pastures shine.

Stopping at the tricycle, Moore asks Catherine to reach out and guess what it is.

Not quite understanding, Catherine lifts the blindfold from her eyes – an old school tie belonging to her father. She looks at her tricycle and, in the shock of it all, she begins to at once grin and cry.

To this, her mother smiles. 'Happy Birthday, my dear,' she says, as she hunkers down and gives Catherine a kiss.

Catherine jumps onto the tricycle and circulates the three adults. Moore chuckles, while reaching for a cigarette. The pedals run free of Catherine's feet, so Elizabeth places her daughter's feet back on and, with the clicks of the wheels building into squeaks, Catherine begins to understand, and she pushes herself further away from her mother and father, propelling herself across the room and into the foot of an empty hatstand in a long rectangle of sunlight.

They all return outside to the farmyard and within minutes Catherine is cycling manically around, veering towards the terrified chickens and the broad black puddles, and she soon learns, if she back-pedals with enough force, how to come to a halt.

Gilbert, looking on at this scene, a hand on his belly, leans towards his younger brother and says that he is leaving soon for Guernsey.

'And have you told Mother?' asks Moore.

'I don't think she'd care,' he replies, 'but, in any case, I'm taking the boat from Dublin Port in two days.'

'I may travel with you, so,' says Elizabeth. 'I've some business to take care of in London.'

Moore looks sidelong at Elizabeth.

Later that evening, Elizabeth and Moore quietly discuss Moore's will at the large dining-room table. Moore agrees to postpone the final wording of the will for a year on the proviso that, in the interim, they try to beget a son. Failing this, Elizabeth agrees to sign this lopsided will that hands eighty per cent of the property to Moore's mother, then, upon her death, to a nephew-in-law one county over and in training to be a vet.

That night, after these gentle discussions, Moore and Elizabeth congress earnestly in their marital bed.

2.

Dr Alois pulls a roasting chicken leg from the stove. Behind him, his dark-haired visitor sits sipping the last of a gin and tonic, while reading from her host's lined notebook. She is unsure where most of his latest paragraphs are leading – they seem more like reminders than statements, themselves only half-harnessed to any argument. She closes the notebook over and pushes it to one side as Alois serves her a leg of chicken, over which he spills chopped vegetables. He then pours her a glass of white wine – from one of two bottles of Riesling sent from home and that he decided to pop open for this occasion.

After dinner, he tells her that his doctor visited him yesterday with 'rather bad news' about his latest blood tests. He tells her that he has not that long to live.

'Three months, and not much more, Catherine,' he says in his clipped Germanic accent.

Catherine, her eyes suddenly watering, goes to comfort Alois, but he puts out his hand and merely asks her to please not.

'It really is fine, Catherine,' he says. 'I always knew it would end in some way like this.'

After a few moments watching her stem tears from her eyes, he gently unfolds and offers her his blue handkerchief, with which she dabs at her cheek.

He asks her if she will care for him.

'I'd like to stay here in my house for whatever time is available to me, Catherine,' he continues. 'There are a few more things I'm keen to write, and perhaps I'll complete some further diagrams, too.'

Catherine nods, saying, 'Of course I will, Alois.'

He pours another helping of wine, as Catherine lights a cigarette and smokes it in deep draws. Gazing out the window, she asks Alois if he is in any pain, to which he merely smiles, and to avoid answering any further, he stands, goes to his pantry and returns with a bottle of sherry. He pours two tiny glasses, then he sits and gazes at the light playing across them. Catherine looks to Alois, then out the window at three birds wheeling over and back on upturnings of air. The clock ticks on the wall to their right as the roof above creaks in the eddies of passing sea gusts.

As Alois gazes at the swirls of his sherry, he imagines the first few moments after his last breath. He pictures a slim pathway leading into a dense forest at the foot of a mountain. He imagines walking that path would be similar to walking along a corridor at night – darkness leading into darkness – and then it occurs to him that this track, as it shrinks to nothing, will almost certainly be uphill, and perversely will prove a struggle to take.

'Shall we go out for a walk and some fresh air, Alois?' asks Catherine, stubbing out her cigarette.

'I'd like that, C; let's,' replies Alois.

At the far end of the strand, Catherine and Alois walk a few feet apart, while to their right the sea laps up onto the shore in tired lines of froth.

Both carry their shoes. Then, at times, they splash along shin-deep in the chilly surf. At the end of a length of rock in the far distance, a tree leans landward, and some miles beyond, as if clinging to the loamy soil, stands the old Belt Ness lighthouse, built one-hundred years before. To the north-east, and way out of sight on a lone crag in the sea, stands the oldest lighthouse on this coast, the Hugo Ness, built another fifty years before the Belt Ness. The remains of a foreman, the Bachelor Brown, is still on this crag. He died six months before its completion when he was struck over the head by the wrought-iron frame for the lighthouse lamp, it swaying chaotically from the delivery boat on a day of high winds. His fellow workers left his remains in a cave on the island and covered the entrance over with a large boulder. For years afterwards, every Easter Sunday, a junior tradesman, who worked on that lighthouse and witnessed its first beam of light, visited the since-abandoned crag to see if the boulder had ever moved.

Catherine and Alois, making their way along the shore, criss-cross and criss-cross once again, until the figure to the left, Alois, begins to list, then stagger. He falls. Catherine runs to him, sinking to her knees. She takes his head into her lap, carefully asking if he is OK. He nods and assures her he needs only to lie down for a moment to catch his breath.

'It all usually passes,' he says.

Some minutes later, she helps him to his feet, and they walk back up the darkening strand, he leaning on her, his arm around her neck and shoulder, like a drunken sailor, and she, a sturdy-seeming support, leans into him, holding him aloft, her arms around this chest, which heaves dangerously as they go. They fall to the ground once, then twice – a puff of sand and a tangle of limbs.

Catherine looks around hopelessly, her dark hair blowing into her broad and fair face, to see if there is anyone there to help. The night begins to set in around them and the lights in the far distance come up. Then Alois regains his senses and stands once more, and they begin to walk back up the dusky beach, over the navy dunes and on towards his timber house.

Lights come on in the ground- and first-floor rooms as lamps are lit.

Then, off out at sea, a drift of low-hanging cloud obscures the head of the Belt Ness lighthouse, giving this cloud the appearance of a great sea fire floating through the air.

I.

Young Catherine, standing by an upstairs window, puts her index finger to the plane of glass. It's a bright and dewy morning and she is looking out over their front lawn, a stone wall and a front gate. On the road beyond, an automobile stalls, issuing plumes of smoke up into the forest-lined sky. Gilbert and Elizabeth step into the rear of the auto, while Moore, thrusting his hands into his blazer pockets, turns from them and makes his way back towards the house.

Catherine's grandmother appears beside her and leads her downstairs, where they meet Moore crossing the corridor. He tousles Catherine's hair before he enters the sitting room and, returning his watch to his pocket, takes a seat at his desk and lights a cigarette, the first of many in his day.

Catherine is led out through the kitchen, into the sun-warm yard and up to a couple of red-headed girls, the O'Haras, waiting at the yellow rear gate. These girls are eight and eleven years of age, pleasant and respectful of their elders, and they take Catherine from the grandmother, who places a sod of turf into the eldest girl's hand to put with her own.

'Be good, now, for the master at school!' she calls, to which the girls nod and wave.

The sun comes and goes as the three young children progress along the edge of the swaying forest, across fields dotted with weary livestock and up a rutted lane to a small white schoolhouse, outside of which is parked the headmaster's car, while underneath a large oak leans Master Francis's high nelly.

At the back door, the children hand their sods of turf to Master Francis, a smiling and fair-haired man. He leads them into the smaller of two large classrooms, where he sits and pulls some books from his bag while instructing these three young children to take their places.

Master Francis then steps to the window, where he looks out over the fields of deep green and the lake in the distance. The night before, he received a message from the daughter of the butcher, Clare, asking him if he was going to the dances, *any Saturday night soon at all?*

Meanwhile, across the county, the lanky blond photographer crouches inside a red phone box at a crossroads two miles from the old apartment he rents in the town of B_. He explains with some anxiety down the phone to Moore Carolan that the family portraits he took were destroyed while he was transporting the plates back to the darkroom in his apartment.

'They must have got exposed along the way!' he says into the handset.

Moore shifts his weight at the window in his front porch, looking on at a murmuration of birds disintegrating into a distant chestnut tree.

'Will you retake them without charge, Mr Austin?'

The photographer, Austin, pauses.

Moore puts his fingers to his forehead.

'I'll pay for your petrol, so.'

Austin, leaning against the wall of the phone box, smiles, revealing a set of crooked and unkempt teeth.

'Very good, sir,' he says. 'Thank you. And when might it suit you and your good family?'

'My wife is away for six days.'

'Shall I come this day week, sir?'

'Very well, and good day, Mr Austin!'

2.

Alois rises from his bed, fully clothed, and closes over the window. He sits at his desk and takes out his lined notebook, lifts his pencil and stalls a moment, nib in the air, as he realises that he has lost sight once again of what moments before had come so clearly to mind.

Downstairs, while Catherine is chopping vegetables for their midday meal, an apple blossom to the rear of her first school comes to her mind. She used to walk past it each morning. She tries to picture her old schoolteacher, Master Francis: Where might he be now? she wonders.

Then, from above, comes a bang and a shudder of joists. Catherine runs up the stairs and knocks on Alois's bedroom door, where inside she hears whimpering.

'Herr Doktor!?' she calls. 'Herr Doktor!?'

And, from the weakness of his whimpering, she decides to ignore the usual civilities and enters.

Alois is sitting on his bed, but his table has been turned over and across the ground are strewn his notebooks and pencils, a steel ruler, a fountain pen and an upturned bottle of black ink. The ink pools across the floorboards, spilling into the cracks, more spreading towards his notebooks. Catherine lifts the papers from the floor, but onto one page a Rorschach-like form has already spread. She shakes the notebook out, speckling her apron and the shoulders of her pristine white blouse with tiny black stars. She lifts the ink bottle, rights the table and shuffles the notebooks and papers back onto its surface. She then steps to Alois and kisses him on the forehead.

Without looking up, he says, 'Perhaps, in the absence of any of mine, we could discuss some of your new thoughts over lunch?'

She pauses at the door to see if there was any heat, any resentment in his utterance.

He casts his ragged handkerchief onto what remains of the ink on the floor, and at this she returns downstairs, lights the candle on the table and finishes preparing her vegetable broth.

Some hours later, and after closing over a navy notebook containing reminders to herself on Thomas Bayes' old theorems on probability, Catherine opens out a green notebook, the one she is attempting to devote to thoughts away from mathematics, and she imperfectly translates from French to English a passage from a book she recently took out on loan from the library of her college – St Hugh's, in Oxford. The book contains a series of lectures given some years before on French public radio – by a 'man of brilliance' called Merleau-Ponty.

... this leaves knowledge of the natural world riddled with gaps, which is how poetry creeps in, she writes. And she places her pencil back down.

It was during the middle years of the war that she deputised as a trainee nurse, and Alois as a porter, at Guy's Hospital in London. The two of them bided at night in the bomb shelters far beneath the hospital, and it was here that they grew to know each other and, in their own strange and at times awkward way, became close. During these at times terrifying nights, Alois told her about his family – three sisters and two brothers – who, with his aged parents, ran a vineyard outside a small South-Tyrolean village called Kaltern. One night, he described to Catherine how, in his late twenties, he'd feared for his life in this mountainous village overlooking a sparkling lake – because it was ceding control at a rampant rate to a handful of emboldened fascists. He told her of his great friend, Peters, who, when caught one night smuggling a batch of anti-fascist pamphlets into the district, had been hauled into the public square, where he was beaten so badly with sacks of sand by this group of local *squadristi* that his jaw was shattered to pieces. 'Brutes,' Alois told her, his blue eyes watering. He went on, his voice often catching with emotion, to tell Catherine how Peters' jaw realigned so poorly afterwards that he could no longer pronounce his own Christian name: Günthram. After this, given his close association with Peters, and with the growing suspicion towards those who spoke German in the area, it became clear to Alois that he had little option but to flee.

Some nights later, in this same bomb shelter, he told Catherine about that day, in late 1929, when he finally left home, and while passing through Bolzano's new train station he noticed these frightful effigies that were being fitted into the base of a new fountain there: 'Satirical sculptural heads of a Black man and a Jew,' he said. The message, he told Catherine, was obvious: that 'them and their kind' were now a new sort of ogre, setting out 'to poison our Christian waters'. He told her that he took the next train to Vienna and had not returned to Italy, Tyrol, or his family since.

By this time, in the late twenties, Alois had capitalised on a paper that had been circulated among some in the Vienna Circle. It was called *Coefficients and Truth Value*, and was a short if piercing pamphlet he wrote about coefficients in aeronautic modelling, and how these coefficients, he reasoned, could be correlated to 'logical atoms' in sentences that are verifiable, and from there 'multiplied out' to the world of scientific meaning and use. It was on the back of this inventive paper that he was invited by an excitable chain-smoking Englishman called Ayer to Oxford to give tutorials to undergraduates in the foundations of mathematics and philosophy. And it was here, he told Catherine, that he completed his final 'turning away' from the aeronautic engineering that had once entranced him so thoroughly in his youth, and he settled instead 'wholly into the games of linguistics'.

On adjacent makeshift chairs in a cramped corner of the shelter in the catacombs beneath London's streets, he began in the quiet of the late evenings to teach Catherine German, and some Italian too, but, because in his home town German was the mother tongue, it was in this language he thought and wrote. As he taught her, by candlelight, beneath the at times shaking ground, Catherine came to enjoy the strange shapes the German language produced in her mind and she admired the frosty aloofness of its grammar, too. But what she liked most was how the rules of this grammar so consistently met the sentences and how one could trace the altering lineages of causation through the fabric of a sentence depending on its tense, the position of its subject, the direction of movement of an object, or if this object was a possession, and suddenly in a sentence containing a feminine noun, the definite article *die* would click, as if behind it lay a dial, into a *der*. She enjoyed these machinations happening quietly beneath the sentences and she grasped the almost baroque difficulties of the grammar with what seemed to Alois a painful ease, and soon she was translating some of the writings he produced in the breaks he was afforded in the hospital during the day. And from this she could iron out some of the 'idiomatic inconsistencies' in his English, too, for which he always showed sincere thanks, nodding his head vigorously, saying, 'Yes, yes, how stupid of me … how totally stupid!'

She came to love how brutally critical he was of himself.

Sometimes they spoke about those instances when language tries to express mathematical logic, and she said to Alois that only with the consistent nature of German grammar would one ever consider such an endeavour. 'Surely no one would ever be encouraged to use English in the realm of mathematical logic?' she said.

At other times she began to learn from him the rudiments of how to be lonely in the world. She was attracted to his self-sufficiency, his almost existential neatness. She found the way he held himself in the world – 'like a ball bearing falling through a boiling fluid' – increasingly if wordlessly appealing. She wondered at times if what she felt for him amounted to what people referred to as love. She often told him about her youth, too – the landscapes, the broad unfolding pastures, her old schoolhouse – and what studies in mathematics and logic she would like to pursue back in Oxford after 'all of this'. She told him that she would really like to teach. And he promised her that he would help. And she believed him. They promised each other, too, that if one was ever injured or fell ill, then the other would care for them. It was an arrangement to which both, as immigrants of a kind, agreed immediately. It produced a hidden structure of support around them, where none was before. Catherine soon began to find that these small intimacies that developed between them were the most beautiful if fleeting of objects.

Then, on one peaceful evening, near the end of the war, and while they were sheltering beneath the hospital, now as much out of habit as necessity, Alois, sitting alongside her at a small wooden table, gave her a kiss on the cheek. Catherine, startled, more so at this breaching of himself than at the kiss itself, turned to Alois, and he then kissed her on the mouth. It was the first time she had been kissed in this way and, from the moment his lips left hers, she felt like she could not wait for the next time his lips returned, but, the next morning, in a fit of righteous, almost religious guilt, Alois appeared at Catherine's station in the hospital, dressed absurdly in his three-piece suit and formal bow tie, and he offered her his unreserved apologies for what he'd done.

‘I behaved like a brute,’ he said, his eyes filled with self-disgust.

She replied, with as much reserve as her heart would allow, ‘Please don’t ever apologise to me, Josef, Herr Doktor; I was not in the least offended.’

1.

In the bright country schoolhouse, young Catherine Carolan peers at the blackboard before her onto which Master Francis has just chalked five rows of numbers.

Two blond-haired children, a barefoot boy and a girl, of five and six, sit alongside her. Behind her, two eight-year-old boys sit at their benches, their heads recently shorn for lice, and behind them sit three eleven-year-old girls.

The three most junior children are writing two-digit numerals with their pencils into their copybooks. Catherine, however, has long mastered the counting, to ten thousand. When she first encountered the numbers eleven to fourteen, her small heart raced at this sudden strange straying from pattern, but then she quickly saw the pattern of zero to one to nine to a multiple of one and ten re-establish, and she felt she could then count forever. The earlier pages in her copybook are filled with shapes of simple kinds, and over them she has written in shaky script the words to which these shapes relate: *rectangle*, *triangle*, *circle*, *square* … Her mother, in the evenings, rehearses with her daughter everything Catherine has encountered with Master Francis in school that day. This is how her mother learned her words and numbers too, and it is this she often tells her daughter, by way of encouragement, as they crouch over a book in front of a candle and the cooling fire. Then, the following day at school, Master Francis often has to take Catherine aside and correct these strange pronunciations she has developed overnight from repeating these words after her mother – who says the word 'circle' in her cockney 'say-kuwl', and 'square' as 'skway-ah', and, so as to rectify these strange variations, Master Francis asks young Catherine Carolan to repeat aloud after him the sounds: 'surkul' and 'skwayre'.

The two other children beside Catherine are bright, and this leads at times to gentle shows of competition between them. Master Francis then, at other times, allows the youngest three to play with multicoloured plastic sticks and bindings to the rear of the classroom. He asks them to construct these things called 'skyscrapers'. After they are done, he looks on at their unsteady and slender constructions, and this ignites in him a long-felt desire to up and emigrate to the city of Chicago. Each evening, when he pedals back to the small labourers' cottage he rents five miles outside the town of B_, he imagines himself in the middle of the metropolis of Chicago, looking on at the magical glassy high-rises emerging either side of him as he whizzes along a boulevard, cars passing, well-dressed men smoking cigarettes while strolling, buses thundering by, the metro coursing in labyrinths beneath his bicycle wheels, which descend a dip and screech to a halt, whereupon Master Francis sees before him, across the bog, the shores then the great impassive body of wind-blown Lake Michigan.

He is very fond of Catherine, who he thinks is a kind and generous girl. He has seen how she shares her food and how, one day, she took a cloth band from her hair and passed it to the girl behind, a few years her senior, who had begun, frustrated at her inability to conjugate a verb, to cry. Master Francis could tell that Catherine had seen this kind of comforting gesture a number of times before. He asked himself, is she then from a sad or even a melancholic household?

'Catherine,' he said at the time, 'it's of course kind to offer Marie your band, but it won't, in the long run, be effective. It would be far more effective if Marie were to learn her irregular verbs, and then there'd be no need for such tears or for such ribbons to stem them.'

Catherine looked up at him, unsure if she had angered him, and she took her balled-up band from Marie and pushed it into her dress pocket.

More recently, Master Francis has become aware of Catherine's growing capabilities with numbers. Oftentimes, when he is teaching long division to the ten- and eleven-year-olds, he sees Catherine Carolan peering over at the blackboard as if in a trance, while he demonstrates the movement of numbers up and down and over and back, and how to carry remainders from a division over to the next numeral – disintegrating one number into another, as it were. A few times, he has asked to see her copybook after one of these demonstrations and he has found the series of long divisions written in her shaky script, but otherwise all perfectly copied out inside her book. He's not yet sure if she is merely collecting his demonstrations or if she has knowledge of what he is doing. He asks himself this question often in the evenings: when does collecting of this patterned kind bend itself into knowledge, and what does that moment feel or look like, and is this departing from pattern memorable ... ? And he often wonders, too, does an equalising of the distance between what the teacher knows and what the student knows lead to progress? Or is it necessary to retain these distances, these differences, and is that what *truly* gives teaching its potential? Sometimes he wonders more deeply if he is not merely some hired magician, tricking these children into a useful form of agreement that they can carry forth unthinkingly into their lives. In the last few months, this Catherine Carolan has uttered the strangest of things to him. One day, while they were compiling a school dictionary of common words, he held a drawing of a tulip before his chest and said to the youngest children, 'This is a tulip,' to which Catherine put up her hand and, when he bade her speak, she said, 'No, it's not, sir; it's a picture of a tulip on a piece of paper.' He can already see a certain cleanliness of mind in her and at the same time no awareness of this cleanliness and how it marks her out from the other children, who vary from average of mind to at times slovenly. Or perhaps – he sometimes wonders to himself in his quietest moments – it is as if she can see through, with a naive, almost pre-linguistic clarity, the conceits he must employ to produce this kind of learning. He has mentioned Catherine and her strange abilities to the headmaster, an impatient boor called Foynes, who has merely said, 'Best to keep an eye on her, so.'

2.

After several more hours of peaceful midday work, planning a new set of lectures for the following semester, Catherine closes over her green notebook and, climbing the stairs, makes for Alois's door. She stands there a moment listening, then she calls to him gently, but there comes no response.

Despite the shrill cry of a seabird outside, she can hear him breathe in that deep way of a sound sleeper, and so she enters.

1.

Master Francis looks across the schoolroom at young Catherine Carolan, but she is already silently staring at him. The children around her are now busy transcribing onto their pages lines of poetry.

Master Francis looks away and back, away and back once more, and still Catherine remains silently staring at him.

He lifts a finger to his face and shakes it about, but there is not a flicker of recognition in her expression. He wonders what thoughts or images are forming in this strange catatonia of hers.

He stands and slowly walks around the classroom, taking in the children hunched over their desks as they write and blot their lines of text. He pauses a moment next to Catherine and, peering into her copybook, he sees a strange grid-like drawing with the numbers 21 and 23 split apart and placed alongside sets of horizontal and vertical lines, with two circles and a loop gathering in the nodes of the grid. He soon realises that she is enacting some unfamiliar method for multiplying these numbers.

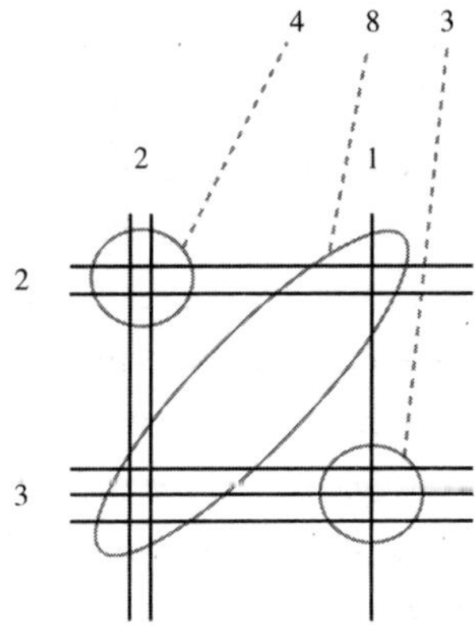

21 × 23 = 483

He set over a dozen of these long-multiplication problems for the older children in the class through the whole of the previous afternoon, and while he looks on at the numbers 21 and 23 and their multiplication sum of 483, he cannot remember if he set them this problem, or if Catherine has merely made it up so as to keep herself occupied.

He taps her on the shoulder and asks what her line drawing is all about, and Catherine looks back up to Master Francis and replies, while pointing at the blackboard, 'Your numbers from yesterday ...'

'Did I write those?' he asks, pointing at the 21 and the 23.

'Yes, sir.'

'And is this how you see numbers, Catherine?' he continues, now pointing to the criss-crossing lines of her shaky little grid.

'Some days …' she says, as her eyes drift out to the tree and its branches, where she counts, in her mind, the points where three branches criss-cross with two then one, and where two more branches criss-cross with two and another one, until a gust of wind then lifts them all apart.

Master Francis looks at Catherine for some moments, until her dark eyes move back to him, then they drop, and she silently returns to her transcription on the opposite page.

'Well, that's very good, Catherine,' says Master Francis before he steps away and returns to the head of the room, where he sets about preparing an afternoon of Irish grammar for the oldest grouping of children in the class.

2.

Catherine takes a seat alongside the sleeping Dr Alois and she looks over his clothing, observing his broad cotton trousers, his brown leather belt and his shirt with its handsomely sewn neck design. He told her once that this rectilinear stitching pattern was particular to his 'realm of South Tyrol'. He told her that the pattern matches the way in which certain roofing timbers are woven in the houses in the upper climes of the surrounding mountains near to his home.

She looks at his peaceful face, and the, to her, elegant line running from his dark eyebrow, across the side of his eye socket, down his cheekbone, past his full lips and on to his narrow chin. He pouts a moment as he breathes more deeply and, from this deep breath, his face clenches into a wince, bringing forth the wrinkles at his eyes. His body tightens as if someone has turned a screw in him, and at this Catherine takes his hand in hers; then she lifts it to her mouth and kisses it.

She steps from his room, the wind picking up outside, and she descends the stairs to the table, the candle and her notebooks once more.

She picks up her clutch pencil and writes into the navy notebook the sentence, *All whole numbers share the twin characteristics of being a. an independent object, and b. one greater than their predecessor.* Then she lifts her pencil to her lips and considers the implications of this thought for the whole number of zero, and if she were to put 'zero' into the set of 'whole numbers' then the formulation she decides that she would have to write would be, *All whole numbers share the characteristics of being a. an independent object, and b. one less than their successor … i.e.* $3 - 1 = 2$; $2 - 1 = 1$; $1 - 1 = 0$.

She turns to the last page in her notebook, then turns it upside down. Whenever a parallel thought appears in her mind, she jots these *pockets of idea*, as she calls them, on the reverse side of the notebook at hand, as if by doing so the progression of thinking from either side of the notebook might provide to her a pincer movement of a kind, closing in on an original thought. On the reverse page of the notebook, she writes, *What might the machinery around a number-object be if installing such a thing allowed for logical operations to be carried out using valid procedures of a step-by-step kind? And how might this logical machinery then touch the number-object?*

She turns the notebook back to the earlier page and she writes, *What theory of numbers might support this act of distinction-making?* And after some pensive moments she writes in capitals beneath it: *THERE MUST BE AGREEMENT BETWEEN PEOPLE AS TO WHAT THE NUMBERS REFER TO, OTHERWISE THE ENTERPRISE MIGHT TURN INTO MERE SOLIPSISM.*

Then, pausing a moment between flipping her notebook over once more or deeming her next thought to belong to this side of the discovery, she puts her pencil to her lips, wets the nib unselfconsciously with the tip of her tongue and writes onto the lines below, *The content of this distinction-making ought to be linked to the number-objects 0, 1, 2, 3, 4, 5 … etc. with a kind of logic that is independent of our minds.*

She places the splayed navy notebook alongside her closed-over green one and realises that what she is beginning to produce here between these two notebooks is a sort of larger inner dialogue.

A gust of wind shudders the kitchen window. Catherine looks up, her eyes returning to the world, and she realises the range and fire to her left has become cold, so she rises, opens the door to it and stokes what remains of the embers within.

1.

The photographer, Austin, steps from his Model T, makes his way through the front entrance of his boarding house and climbs the four shadowy flights of stairs – his long legs clapping out three steps at a time – until he arrives at the door to his lodgings.

The last family who lived on this floor vacated in a rush, over a year ago, leaving errant pieces of silver cutlery and items of expensive furniture – a dressing table, a Victorian drinks trolley, an armchair. His landlord has told him that the father was escaping 'a rather large' gambling debt – 'all frittered away on the nags' – and that this family now work on a farm holding in the northern districts of rural Texas.

The upper floor is bright and dry, but crowded over with Austin's photography equipment and a drawing table alongside which dangle, from a line of red nylon, fifteen photographic prints depicting a wealthy family one county west of B_, all celebrating the christening of a set of enormous twins.

Austin's grandmother, who died almost three years before while nursing young rebel soldiers on a sodden lake island, often called him, when he was in his teens, 'a man of trajectories, a man always aiming to be elsewhere ... and agitating to a state of betterment!' He could never quite tell if this, in her eyes, was a good or bad thing.

His interests roam and the ones he alights on quickly become obsessions, for sometimes years on end. In his late teens he worked as a railway linesman in the mid-western districts and memorised the locations of all crossings, over bridges, under bridges and huts, especially those used by the British army for stockpiling tools and explosives for tunnelling. In the years up to independence, he sold this information on to a local rebel captain, who became pro-Treaty and who years later made great use of this information while he and a small number of young local men were on the run from the British army, avoiding forced conscription. It was with this money that Austin bought a stretch of domestic bog and a horse and cart with which he soon began to sell turf in the surrounding towns, and in his spare time he played handball at the local GAA clubs. He excelled at both. Days after his largest turf sale, he won a county handball championship, displaying 'great coordination and strength, for such a long lad'. Then, satisfied to near boredom with what he'd achieved from turf sales and handball, his attention roved once more and alighted with a deep curiosity on photography and golf. After the height of the civil war passed, and for his inadvertent hand in his younger brother's maiming and death, he – now 'nothing but a filthy Free-Stater' – was advised by his mother to leave his home and not darken 'so much as the county-bounds' ever again. From the seasonal sales of turf, he had made enough money to purchase a camera, his second-hand auto and for a rental deposit for this boarding-house accommodation. Since then, he has lived alone, trying and failing often to find female companionship. Some nights, with his long frame bent into his undersized bed, he cries himself to sleep.

Austin, pushing a lank strand of blond hair from his brow, steps over to the line of photographs and inspects their condition. He unclips four and brings them to his drawing board, where he slips them into a stiff cardboard envelope that he closes over and places onto the drinks trolley by the door. He removes the remaining photographs from above the table and puts them into a filing cabinet, upon which lies a large scroll of paper that he lifts, removing from it an elastic band and releasing his curling drawings.

He is in the throes of designing a golf course and the drawing he opens out is a schematic of the eighteenth hole – 'The Elms' – belonging to a course he imagines building on a stretch of prime farmland overlooking a lake. He takes out a smaller drawing, made on tracing paper, of the whole golf course, practice area and clubhouse, and he places it over an Ordnance Survey map denoting this preferred stretch of farmland that has for over a decade now belonged to Moore Carolan. Each hole in this layout is designed in relation to the contours of the land, the lake, the existing trees. And, within each design, Austin has made more detailed drawings showing the tee-boxes, the fairways, their drainage, and the shapes and undulations of the greens and surrounding bunkers. He has also designed the flags and the dynamic font for the numbers on each flag – numbers he saw one afternoon while passing a door to a fancy hotel in Dublin. On each of the eighteen holes, he has at least one bunker designed in the outline of an internal body part: a kidney, a lung, a spleen … And every green playfully approximates, sometimes in repetition, to the twelve inland counties of Ireland. Oftentimes, late at night, when his mind begins to slow, and when those rivulets of family guilt begin to trickle, he suddenly gets to his feet and, at his drawing board, he looks over these designs while writing out on a sheet of paper the number of a hole on this course, and underneath he invents and lists the climactic conditions of the time (wind direction, speed, humidity, recent volume of rainfall, temperature) and, with this in mind, he draws in the lightest of pencil lines the curvatures of what the perfect drive, iron shot and putts would look like over this course. He then describes, in short lines of prose, the perfect way to play each hole under a chosen set of weather conditions, the best state of mind for each shot and the degree to which one should feel confidence or caution. From this, he is closing in on the value of difficulty – the stroke index – of each design. Most evenings of late, he has played his golf course imagining a stiff wind coming in off the west-south-west on a sunny day, with an air temperature oscillating around a pleasant seventy degrees Fahrenheit.

As he spreads his latest drawing of the eighteenth hole out on the table, a knock comes at the door. He places four lead weights upon the corners of his drawing, walks to the door and admits his visitor, a skinny youth delivering a telegram from Moore Carolan instructing Austin to come a day earlier from the time first proposed – … *the early return of dear wife from London. Stop.*

2.

Several miles east and along the horizon line of the greying North Sea, a lone Dutch boat chugs its way to a stretch of water where the owners of this boat believe that under the seabed lies a vast reserve of oil. Within a week, this crew of Dutchmen will have scraped scores of samples from the seabed and, within another fortnight, they will have received results as to the chemical make-up of these samples and these results will tell them that these rocks and stones contain such a high level of carbon that beneath them must lie a second sea, but one full of oil and natural gas. These Dutchmen will go to a stevedore's bar in the harbour in Aberdeen and drink for a week, then, sick as dogs, return across the North Sea to Rotterdam and prepare their enormous plans for this oil's extraction.

Herr Doktor Alois rouses from a dream, instantly vanished. He approaches his window while rubbing his face. His blue eyes scan the seascape beyond, where he sees through a light rain the outline of a sturdy sea vessel chugging north with what looks like a gantry crane atop. He imagines, within the boat, the unpleasant heaving to and fro.

He rubs his neck and wonders where these dreams of his go to when they vanish, or is this the only absolute feeling we can ever have on Earth – the sudden extinction of dreams. He sleeps more now than he has ever slept before, and yet his face is drawn out with exhaustion.

When he was a younger man and first studying aeronautics in Bolzano, he could, drunk on his fascination for the subject, get by for weeks on end with three or four hours of sleep a night. There were days, too, some years after this, as he began pivoting from his studies in aeronautics to linguistics and logic, when his enthusiasm for his subject was such that, in the evenings, he'd nearly resent the raw physiological need for sleep. The last time he felt such vitality in his life was over four summers in the mid-thirties, when he would travel up from Oxford to this coastal site south of Aberdeen and its grand old distant Grampians. He'd give the entire four months of these holiday breaks over to the building of this house. The first two summers, he brought a large canvas tent with him, in which he slept and ate when he was not working. By the third summer, he had enough of the house erected to sleep rough indoors. During the winters, back in Oxford, he loved dreaming and inventing the next steps required to complete his building, which he called, to himself, *Haus Alois*. These days, though, just before he falls asleep, he wonders if he will wake up at all and what his last dream-thought deep in this night of his mind might be, and might this image he produces in there be something that accompanies him to breathless purgatory – a purgatory he most associates, for some reason he cannot fathom, with an all-encompassing sensation of airless thirst.

He turns to his desk and writes into his lined notebook the word *kite* and, alongside it, the words of the materials he will need to construct it:

wooden dowels
wire
cloth
twine

He begins to sketch out a cuboidal kite, similar to the one he made with his dear old friend, Peters, those decades ago. He calculates the weight and surface area of this thing and, from this, the wind-speed required to lift an object of this kind into the air: twenty-five to twenty-seven miles per hour. The calculations come easily to him and within minutes he is attributing dimensions, accurate to a centimetre, to the plan, elevation and cross sections of his kite. Realising that he will need either glue or screws for the joints, he calculates the weight of sixteen small steel screws (six grams), then the weight of a ten-metre-long strip of glue (three grams). To the right, he lists out a final inventory of materials:

4 × dowels – 2 m in length each
8 × dowels – 0.5 m in length each
Cloth (a light nylon) – 2 m × 4 m
Glue – 1 pot
String – 40 m, red
Wire – (aluminium, 0.1 mm diameter) 5 m
Thread – one spool

He copies out the inventory from his notebook onto a loose sheet of paper, then takes the stairs down to Catherine, who is reclined on the couch, reading a now well-thumbed book on modern logic, which she closes over as he enters. She looks up and remarks on how pale he is. She asks if he slept 'at all well' the night before.

'I slept for an age,' he replies in that odd way of his, as if announcing an aphorism for transcription.

She makes to stand, but he instead advances towards her, asking, 'Would you mind terribly, the next time you go to town, Catherine, putting these items onto your list?'

He hands her the slip of paper and Catherine squints at the writing.

'Very well,' she says.

Alois returns upstairs and lies down once more. The dunes in the distance shake in the wind and drizzle.

Catherine walks to the table and looks out the kitchen window. The far-off inland trees bend. She has crumpled up his list and it lies in a ball on the table. She was unable to read a word of what her host had written. Alois has asked her to purchase many of these mysterious lists of items over the last two weeks and she has purchased none of them, and he has never pursued it. She hopes this list of illegible whims will also turn out to be forgotten.

I.

Austin stands in a ragged door opening, his legs and arms spread wide. He'd broken through his apartment wall the evening before. He's trying to decide if he should smoothen it down and fit a door to it, but after walking over and back from kitchen to drawing office and through the doorway to his new photography studio, he realises that he likes this strange portal and that he enjoys the uninterrupted flow between the objects and fluids from all three domains – tea, ink, oil – and how the scents of one domain can drift into and perhaps even affect the other.

Austin's tripod leans against the wall at the entrance to his apartment, alongside his camera and a gleaming box of plates, all of which he now gathers up and carries carefully down to his automobile on the broad and empty street below.

He drives for half an hour, towards the farm of Moore Carolan. He speeds along a rough trunk road that runs some miles parallel to the small district village where Clare Dargan now works.

*

As he bends to his tripod in Carolan's farmyard, he realises, looking down the lens once more, that this young dark-haired daughter is now less suspicious of him and his tripod and camera. Moments before, she tried to include her tricycle in the photograph, but Moore – tiring of her tawdry insistences – leaned towards her and clipped her across the ear. Catherine looked at her father a moment, touching her lobe, her lip trembling, but she knew, or at least it seemed she'd learned, that this was not the time to cry.

She turns to the camera and frowns, as her mother, father and grandmother stiffen again into their familial pose, and with this Austin exposes a plate, and, looking up at the light, asks them to 'Stay as ye are for one more there, please.' He slides a new plate in and carries out another exposure, through which Catherine's face transforms from a frown into a smile. He stands back from the camera and thanks the family for their patience.

'Not at all, Mr Austin,' calls Moore, as Catherine makes away on her tricycle, scattering hens, while Moore approaches Austin and invites him to join 'my good wife and me for a drop of afternoon tea'.

2.

It has since begun to rain again, but this time more heavily than before.

Alois stands from his table and, at his bedroom window, he looks out over the shaking dunes, the path, the row of beach bungalows and the sea thrashing, off in the distance.

Catherine, meanwhile, downstairs, upon hearing the rapping of the raindrops at the kitchen window, makes from her seat to the back garden with a large wicker basket in her arms.

The stubby candle she lit some minutes before waves woozily in the tiny drafts circulating the room. Out the back window, Catherine can be seen struggling through the rain as the clothes line lifts and swings, and as the white shirts, undergarments and a sheet – with a faint red circle in its middle – shift and tangle. She unclips the sheet, shoves it into her basket, pushes her dark hair from her face and disappears for a moment from view. Then, she bursts in through the kitchen entrance, the door swinging in the squall behind.

The candle flame stretches and flickers into nothing; from it a line of smoke appears that shivers into a tapering sine-wave of vapour.

Catherine slams the door shut, pulls the damp items out of the wicker basket, folds them on her raised knee and places them onto a railing above the range.

She straightens out her hair, catches her breath and pours herself a cup of water before she returns to her green notebook, now containing the beginnings of this new set of lectures she is working on. After some time absent-mindedly flicking over and back between the pages, she notices the candle flame has been extinguished. She leans forward and relights it. She lifts her pencil to her lips and touches the nib with her tongue. Then she puts the pencil down and begins to think, for a moment, of her father and his remains now lying in a graveyard overlooking a lake in the middle of her home county. She pauses for almost a minute and she begins to think of her mother, now ensconced in her grandparents' cottage, way south in Hoxton, London, and her pottering about, most likely, or perhaps just sitting at a kitchen table, too, in a similar pose, chin in hand, and thinking of her daughter thinking of her. Catherine considers the perished connection between herself and her mother, and she realises that this stemmed from years of them both not knowing what to say to one another; this ragged silence had grown from two unspoken feelings of blame held up at a distance to each other, like mirrors signalling across a quiet valley – blame for the demise of her father at his own hand, decades ago. Then, unable to remember even the last thing she might have said to her mother during her last visit to London, she lifts her pencil once more and returns to making these notes in her green notebook. Within these pages she is sketching out a set of ten two-hour lectures for the upcoming semester, the aim of which, at this early stage at least, is to put questions to her students on how a person might describe the relationship between mathematical probability and the world it models, in moments of both success and failure. As she reads her scribbles and seemingly random thoughts, she realises in these new models of probability she is developing that she is not so interested in how the mathematical accuracy of this modelling can be improved, so much as understanding better the irrational fluxes of faith and even belief that she feels must flow through the undersides of the relationship, away from numbers and towards *the self*. She is not quite sure yet how she will best put these questions to her intake of undergraduates, but returning to the type of knowledge gained through the body is where she hopes to slip a wedge and see if she can pry anything open anew to look at with her students. She feels some days that there must be an *optimal position* to be found in this relationship between world and model, and it is from this position, it seems clear to her, that the richest description of what happens there can be produced. She speculates at times if the best route towards these questions is to lift the habits of mathematical thought into other realms of thinking and judging, or to step away from these habits altogether.

It is hard to tell if the creak came first or if Catherine looked up first, but either way she is now looking at Alois pausing on the sixth step of the timber stairway. The top half of his body is in shadow, but his hands at his waist are illuminated.

He opens a hand and asks Catherine if she has remembered to bring him his things from town.

'Which things?' she asks.

'The kite, chief amongst them,' he replies.

'Oh,' she says, surprised. 'A kite?'

He shifts his weight on the stairs as he takes hold of the maple banister.

'I must have forgotten,' she says. 'I can fetch it next time I visit.'

'When will that be?'

'Tomorrow?'

'And why not today, Catherine?'

'Of course,' she replies, writing the word *kite* in the top right-hand corner of her notebook. 'I will leave once the rain stops.'

'Of course,' replies Alois, and he returns to his bedroom, where he slips his trousers from his thinning hips and sits once more at his desk, crossing his skinny legs one upon the other. He puts his head into his hands for some time, growing frustrated that this day free of pain has brought forth so little progress in his work.

He then turns some pages of his notebook in an attempt to regather his thoughts around where they were leading some days before, but instead he encounters a sketch of a kite, and, on seeing this, he recalls not asking Catherine to purchase for him a kite per se, but the makings of one. He looks over the inventory to the right of the drawings of the kite he designed and recalls that, 'Yes, it was only these *elements* I wanted.' He stands, pulls on his trousers and returns down the stairway to the kitchen to clarify what he had meant, minutes ago, by 'kite', but the rain has cleared outside and Catherine has already left.

If he were standing at his bedroom window looking out over the dunes and the stony pathway between them and the line of new bungalows adjacent, he'd see her walking away from his house, and if he could somehow bend his view so he could see her broad and handsome face, he would note that it is lined with tears.

He approaches the table and lifts the cover of her notebook for a moment, taking in her familiar scribbles and rounded glyphs; then he closes the notebook over, licks the tips of his index finger and his thumb and extinguishes the candle's flame.

I.

Moore Carolan leads Austin from the back door of his farmhouse and across his yard to the yellow entrance gate.

Moore, now in shirtsleeves, is smiling broadly as he tells Austin all about the upcoming 'inaugural meeting' of a local gun club, which he has helped to found. Squinting in the sun, he says that he would like to secure Austin's services to photograph, 'to record for posterity', this meeting. Austin, barely listening, turns to look at the land that runs down from the farmhouse to the lake. The light plays across its surface as some trees heave over and back along the shoreline in a strong lake breeze. Austin imagines this land before him as the third, fourth, fifth and fifteenth holes of his golf course. His eyes glaze over as he visualises a golfer in the distance, readying to strike with a six iron a ball onto a green in the shape of the county of Leix – a green that slopes steeply from right to left, down towards the water. The distant golfer takes a three-quarter swing, sending the ball high into the air, slicing through the currents of wind before its climb stalls and the ball begins to fall. It pitches onto the front quarter of the green, but because the imaginary golfer was playing from the rough to the right of the fairway, the ball, lacking backspin, skips forward, speeds past the flagstick with its red-and-green flag (an elegant white number *5*, Austin imagines, embroidered into the fabric), before running through the green, between two deep bunkers and into the rocks that topple down to the lapping lake water. Austin smiles as he imagines this distant golfer thinking to himself how unlucky he was to get 'such a flyer' out of the long grass.

'Mr Austin, is that date suitable for you?' asks Moore Carolan, hitching with his thumb a trouser brace up over his shoulder.

'The date, sir?'

'The fifteenth, at five p.m.'

'Oh. Of course, sir. Let me make a mental note!'

'And do you shoot?' asks Carolan.

'Just pictures, sir!'

'And I saw in the newspaper,' chuckles Carolan, 'that you played expertly in the Ferns Cup last week. Four and three, no? It must have been satisfying to settle the tie so early.'

'I won, five and four in the end, sir,' replies Austin. 'It began to rain over the back nine and our coastal friends were not so slick on the heavier turf. We made it into the next round, in any case.'

Austin, touching a button on his worn-out navy blazer, then turns from the lake, rubs Catherine's head as she glides past, and shakes her father's hand.

'The gun club on the fifteenth it is, so.'

2.

The crepe blue-and-white paper tail of a diamond-shaped kite trails up after Catherine Carolan as she ascends the stairs.

She raps on the bedroom door until Alois gets to his feet. She can hear his bedsprings creak.

He answers the door with a vacant expression on his narrow pale face, and looking to Catherine says, in that abrupt and clipped way of his, 'I stink.'

Catherine leans forward and inhales.

'Shall I make you a bath, Alois?'

'Please, Catherine; that would be nice.'

He looks to her hands, and she passes him the kite.

'Is this what you meant, Alois?'

He frowns and takes the blue-and-white thing in his hands, looks it over and says, 'Not quite, but it shall have to do.'

An hour later and a red-cheeked Catherine is once more at Alois's bedroom door. There comes no answer to her series of playful knocks – *pa pa pap pap pap*. Behind her, the bathroom door lies open, framing a steaming bathtub, three-quarters way filled with soapy water.

'Your bath, Herr Doktor,' she calls through the door.

On hearing his bare feet upon the floorboards, she takes the stairs down and returns to her seat at her books and her notes. She sighs, having grown tired of the demands of his lower moods. She takes a sip from her glass of water and then looks up from her reading at the sound of his feet thumping across the corridor, followed by the slipping and sliding of his body as he lowers himself into the water. She goes to the stove, where she lifts a bubbling pot of vegetable broth and places it to the right, away from the heat.

A gigantic thud comes from upstairs and down through the floorboards cascade drips, lines, then shredded planes of soapy water. She gasps, runs to her table and lifts her books and notes to the couch, then she chases upstairs to find Alois lying on the floor, naked, his brown towel around his shins, and behind him his overturned bathtub, its metal base shining lozenge-like in the evening sun.

With great strain, she lifts his upper body with her arm angled around his shoulders and ribs. And as her right hand grasps at his wet torso, she pictures suddenly her father's body being lifted by four workmen off the floor of their outhouse, minutes after she'd found him one afternoon, having returned from school; he'd been slumped on the ground alongside an empty bottle of whiskey and a spilt jar of pills. She and Alois stagger across the landing and into his bedroom. She eases him onto his bed, then she places her blushing cheek above his mouth. Once she feels a few distant puffs of his breath on her skin, she turns and makes off towards the bathroom, lifts his sodden towel from the floor, wrings it and casts it out into the landing. After some attempts, she rights the bath up onto its four stubby legs, but as she makes to leave, she slips, falling onto her back and striking, with a *dong*, the base of her skull on the lip of the tub.

She lies there motionless.

As the water drips and drops, and the building quietly creaks around them, her breathing and the breathing of Herr Doktor Alois fall into then slowly out of resonance. The light outside collapses a few degrees as the breeze eases into near stasis; two birds fly past Alois's bedroom window, then reappear in the half-steamed-over window of the bathroom. Then, these birds disappear in elongated twists of flight into a broad chestnut tree in bloom inland, at the base of which stand men with axes.

Catherine rouses, lifting her head from the bathroom floor. The blood from her wound has puddled into what is left of the bath water, turning it brown as it drips from the ceiling of the kitchen and onto the table below.

She stands and looks around herself for almost a minute.

'Och,' she says, remembering where she is.

She feels for the back of her head to see if her wound is still bleeding.

She goes downstairs and brings a bucket and mop back up, and begins to clean, before returning downstairs to wipe off the table and mop the floor here too. Then she takes her hand mirror and flips open her purse mirror, and in these sliding reflections inspects the back of her head. Her large brown eyes look askance at the base of her skull and the unruly congealment of her black hair. Her cheeks are now bloodless. She gently washes her hair in a basin by the sink, then wraps a small blue towel around her head.

She returns to Alois's bedroom. He still lies unmoving on his bed, breathing in a way that might be called stertorous. She leans towards him and kisses his cheek. Then she kisses his lips. She looks to his face to see if anything has altered.

She lifts the blue-and-white kite from the foot of the bed and places it onto his table. She fluffs a pillow and eases it beneath his head. She feels his skull for some moments, checking for bumps or grazes. At times, her feeling around his head transforms into a flagrant caress, pushing some of his soft curls back from his brow. Then, gently lifting his two eyelids at once, she peers into his eyes, both brilliantly blue yet unresponsive – as if she has just come upon two frozen-over ice holes deep in an expanse of Arctic land. She lays a sheet over his legs and chest, and begins to pull the curtains. As she stands by the window, looking out through the long slit of light between the curtain fabrics, surveying the dunes, the pathway and the row of beach bungalows arrowing away into the near distance, Alois opens his eyes. He lies there awhile, his hands on his chest, looking on at this poorly lit stranger with a long, elegant neck, standing at his window – a stranger who is wearing on her head a blue turban. He believes for a moment that he has been transported many thousands of miles east to a small room in India. He hears cattle low outside, then the faint clang of cowbells. He closes his eyes once more and allows himself to settle. Catherine pulls the curtain to and leaves for downstairs, hungry now for some vegetable soup to which she will add a thick slice of buttered bread.

I.

Master Francis stands at the blackboard and writes out in large chalk strokes the numerals:

4,500 / 15 =

He turns back to the three older girls, all from an O'Shea family who run a small tillage and mixed livestock farm two miles south of the schoolhouse, and he says, 'From what I demonstrated yesterday, girls, can you please divide four thousand, five hundred by fifteen, and please show your work.'

To this, the three girls bow their heads, dip their ink and, with gently rustling sounds floating up from their pages, they transcribe these numbers into their copybooks, blot them, then lift their pencils and begin to compute. Master Francis looks to young Catherine Carolan, but her eyes are fixed on the board. Then she looks away and writes in her shaky script the number *300* into her copybook.

Master Francis, with squeaking chalk, writes onto the board two more formulations of far larger and stranger numbers, and, without looking at the students again, he takes his seat. With a strike of a match, he lights a cigarette. Catherine looks once more to the board and, in the following moments, writes onto the back cover of her copybook the numbers *57* and *46*, the results of the complex long divisions neatly inscribed by her teacher.

From the room next door emerges the muffled grunt and clap of a child being viciously caned, and to each clap then comes the sound of a stifled reciprocal whimper. And, so as to drown out the sound from these younger children's ears, Master Francis begins to hum a hymn remembered from his altar-boy days called 'Abide with Me'. His humming fills the room.

Once the caning next door has come to an end, he ceases his humming, takes a draw from what remains of his cigarette and asks the two eight-year-old boys to come to his desk and show him their transcriptions of twenty in-tandem lines of Oliver Goldsmith's 'The Deserted Village', a poem all of these children, after their eight years with Master Francis, will be able to recall – 'parent of the blissful hour' – for the rest of their lives. He looks over their smudged copybooks, inspecting the lines and lines of poorly formed joined writing relaying a poem he knows by heart and, at wearisome times of the year – 'Thy glades forlorn confess the tyrant's power' – usually the first few weeks after the clocks go back in October, and as a source of solace, he repeats to himself aloud. He looks for a moment to Catherine, but she has put her pencil down and is now looking out the window at the sunshine and shadows passing through the boughs of the oak tree that shelters and has sheltered for decades this south-facing stone facade of the schoolhouse.

2.

It is some days since the bathtub incident and Catherine is sitting, in her upright and attentive way, at the kitchen table, re-reading lecture four, 'Animal Life', by this scholar Merleau-Ponty. Over the last decade or so, her research, her main body of work, has veered far away from the mathematical logic she studied at first. During this time, she spent a pointless few years engaged with the last paltry works of those logical positivists. She had followed Alois into this terrain, and though its at times pained alliance of 'verifiable sentences' with the deductive methods of the sciences allured her at first, she began soon to look in another direction altogether from all of this. Then, one afternoon, during a long discussion with Alois in his teak and window-lined college office in Keble, it finally occurred to her that all these positivists were doing was scorching out linguistic ground to dissolve the foundations of previous philosophical edifices – *What is Justice? What is Beauty?* – but they had, she said, 'no idea what to put there instead'. At the time, Alois dismissed many of her claims, but she noticed, within a year, the more often they spoke, the less he was concerned with 'the verification of sentences' and the more interested he became in 'a responsibility to meaning'. But now her energies have veered even further away from all of this and towards the world of psychology and perception – especially, now, the perception of animals and madmen.

Herr Doktor Alois, on better days, sits for a while with her in the kitchen, sipping tea, and he quizzes her on why she is entering into such a field of study. He has spent the last few years working in what he refers to as 'linguistic philosophy' and he has tried to draw Catherine in too, but so far she has resisted.

'Is there not enough in trying to understand what we say, us humans to each other, and what that might tell us about what we perceive?' he last asked.

'I've become a little tired of humans, Alois,' she replied, 'especially the ones that claim to be most rational. And I've begun to realise, too,' she said, 'that clarity is a more difficult aim than I'd ever imagined.'

She opens up her navy notebook, the one she has given over to whatever thoughts and fragments of thoughts she has on mathematics these days. She seems to be wavering between two directions: one, the direction of probability, with a view to returning to the studies she carried out years back on the Englishman Thomas Bayes; and the other, a return in the direction of modern logic, with a view to understanding to what extent the removing of *the psychological* from this logic really means only removing its linguistic features and leaving this logic then to a mere silent showing of its procedures. She feels that these are the only two directions in the world of mathematics about which she has any remaining curiosity, but she is unsure about how to step back into these pools of thought ... What she is sure about is that she does not want to step back in the way in which she was first taught. She thinks at times about how drab she found Alois's recently expressed desire to 'tidy up and make neater the borders between concepts'. She feels that Alois has mistaken these new philosophical tools of linguistic philosophy for technique, and this technique, then, for thought ... She feels that any new developments in or between fields of study require the borders between concepts to be kept soft, malleable and prone to rupture. She can feel her instincts at these great depths of specialisation turning bizarrely *humanist*, and she wonders if such an urge is one that will only produce in the end a sense of inner auto-asphyxiation.

Alois is lying asleep upstairs now. He has lost yet more weight. She worries each morning if he will appear at all, or if a sound or a shunt will ever come from his room. The skin around his hips is so tight it shines in the light, and at times in the dark too. At some hours in the night she has heard him stir, light a lamp and sit at his desk. She finds it hard, despite their disagreements and his low moods, to see his lively mind so quickly deteriorate, and with this slowing the lessening of his wit, and the altering of his personality, too.

She looks out the kitchen window and listens to the sea breeze as it whips a blue and a white towel on the line. In the distance, inland, a set of large trees are being cut down for a carriageway that will be completed there in two years' time, connecting the emerging southern suburbs to the outer ring road. She watches these men dismantle a tree until behind it looms up a peak of the smoking dark outline of the city of Aberdeen. She wonders, ought she call Dr Bain in the city once more, to see if he might pay another visit to her host, to see if anything in his bloods has changed, to see if there is any hope at all.

Catherine then pictures her old schoolteacher, Master Francis – 'Amidst thy desert walks the lapwing flies' – he with his hand on her shoulder as he spoke to her encouragingly on her last day of school there.

It was the day before she and her mother packed up and left alone for London. She recalls his eyes being sad. It was near the end of term and Catherine had been recommended to a grammar school, local to her grandparents in London, for the following semester, and some years later she would go on to receive a scholarship to St Hugh's College, Oxford, having excelled in extremis in four A levels: mathematics, physics, Latin and technical drafting. It was at nearby Keble College that she first heard of this Herr Doktor Alois. He was known there to be an elusive sort, not keeping contact hours and rarely seen on the college grounds. He seemed to have no relationship with any of the other lecturers or professors and rarely dressed in the formal college clothing, the gowns and such – clothing that Catherine always found strange, gothic, clerical. Having heard of his long-past work in aeronautics, she decided to send him a short paper on what she saw, while briefly researching this subject, as imprecisions between aeronautical models and the drag coefficients that claim to multiply the dimensions of the models and small test-objects in wind tunnels out towards full-scale reality, full-scale application. She began thinking about these troubling little coefficients while chatting to an undergraduate engineer one morning in the Jenkins Building, not a ten-minute walk from St Hugh's. He was a tall and shy Scottish lad called Straine, who'd met her, as appointed, at the front corner of the building under a pediment statue of a child astride a flying turtle. He had contacted her to see if she might look over the mathematics in his work, to make sure he was not making any 'dodgy moves'. She quizzed this clever Charles Straine about more aspects of aerodynamic modelling, and this all then fed into her informal paper (*a frippery* she thought, long afterwards), composed of these observations, which she sent to Alois. After a while, and with no word, Catherine assumed Alois had either not read her paper or thought it below comment, until one day she received a folded note in her mailbox from Alois, asking her if she could visit his office for a 'further conversation' about her paper. She knew by then, however, that she had nothing more to say on this subject, that she had – to herself, at least – 'bottomed it out'. *Turbulence is only for the gods and birds to understand ... nothing further*, she wrote in her return note – and, instead of keeping her appointment, out of fear, undergraduate timidity, she decided not to go. This only produced more curiosity in Alois to find out who this student of mathematical logic was and why she would be interested in the fragility of coefficients connecting the models of aeronautic experiments to their full-scale counterparts in the real world.

Then, he heard tell of her a few months later, deep into the Michaelmas term of 1937, from an extrovert Austrian economist who had arrived there for the year and had told Alois – with whom he dined often – about this young Irish woman who had argued with extraordinary politeness with a senior lecturer about whether mathematics was a series of discoveries or a series of inventions. The senior lecturer, he told Alois, found her position troubling because he believed like most others that mathematics was a distant corpus from which humanity perpetually mined, hoping someday to reach the core and with it uncover the secrets of a godly universe. Whereas she, 'this pragmatic young Carolan lady', claimed it could not be so, that each 'discovery' was merely an invention 'cloaked in a vain posture of wonder' and that 'the end of our inventions will only demarcate the end of what we as a species can do or imagine with mathematics.' She then went on in what was reported as an unbroken stream of thought, saying that numbers were entities that had been programmed, 'hardwired' into our beings, and in this we have no say other than to be innately able to use them, and such is the depth to which our use of numbers is hardwired into us that, far from considering this a natural gift, we ought as much 'to see this as a curse put on us by a pernicious god,' she said. She finished up her firm if gently made claims with a sentence this Austrian professor had not heard before: 'I think,' she said, 'that the only human aspects, sir, in the world of mathematics are the functions that lie between the numbers – and it is these that are the inventions, and if these are human constructions, then they are all that is in mathematics that can ever, in terms of logic at least, be sublime.'

Alois, when he heard this from the Austrian professor, knew he wanted to meet the elucidator of this bizarre idea as soon as he could.

What he eventually found was a shy, handsome young Irish woman, who spoke with a strange reticence, until he asked her about something not of the world external to her, but more so of her mind, and on this she'd open up and express herself in these streams of complete grammatical sentences, almost as if she had for years spoken only to herself of these things, and not so much composing her thoughts as simply trying to control them. Catherine in turn felt, whenever she spoke with Alois, that he was the person she had been waiting to talk with all her life – the sort of person to whom she could describe without fear the stranger terrains of her thoughts.

1.

Austin brings his Model T to a halt opposite the butcher's on the main street. A blinkered ass pulling an unmanned cart clops past. Austin peers across the road and, when he sees the outline of Clare Dargan placing pale folds of wet offal into the window display, he steps from the auto and crosses over. She looks up as he, smiling, waves to her.

Then comes the tinkle of a bell from above the door as its large glass planes send wan rectangles of reflected sunlight out and back across the colourful facades of the terraced houses opposite.

He asks her how she is today, and Clare replies, peering up at Austin and wiping her greasy hands down on her apron, that she is 'very well, considering'.

'Considering?' he asks.

'Oh, you know,' she says, dropping her eyes.

A local sheep farmer, McGraine, enters and orders five pork chops. Austin steps to one side, nodding at McGraine, a gruff local who drinks milk with whiskey each night until he slumps to sleep in his armchair beside his crumbling open fire, the cool of his cottage then gathering in around him until he stirs near dawn. Austin looks on admiringly at Clare as she pulls the chops from the display case, wraps and weighs them, and asks the farmer, as she pushes a ring of fair hair behind her ear, for two pence.

After McGraine departs, she tidies the display case, easing with her strong and blood-stained fingers large hunks of beef, pork, veal, and white sausages into a makeshift grid. Then she looks up and asks Austin, her green eyes moving up and down and over and back across his angular features, if she can assist him at all.

'A few of your best pork sausages, please!' he says, grinning.

To which she lifts a string of these plump sausages and, hovering her knife at the twist of skin between the fourth and fifth, she looks to him, a dark and flawless eyebrow raised.

Austin nods and, as she gathers the sausages together onto a square of greaseproof paper, he asks her if she'll be at the dance on Saturday night.

She pauses awhile, then says that she will.

'Might your friend, this *Gaeilgeoir*, Francis, be there too?'

'That's his business, I'm sure,' she replies, and she hands Austin the neatly folded packet of meat.

Austin looks at the packet in his hand a moment and then looks up and, in the growing quiet, asks, 'May I photograph you sometime?'

Clare, standing back from the counter, looks away.

'Maybe someday, when I'm more beautiful,' she replies.

The clock behind the counter ticks. Austin looks to her. Her face remains unchanged until she looks to him and says brightly, 'Well, that'll be four pence, so.'

*

Austin, speeding towards a stretch of domestic bog a few miles east of the small town of B_, wonders if his rival Francis is the only impediment between him and this enchanting Clare Dargan. He wonders, is her reticence with him shyness or a lack of interest, or has she already given her heart, as it were, to this blasted teacher from the back arse of the south-west?

His car bangs over a pothole and the whole thing jumps. He winces, then listens out for the next hundred yards for the sound of a loosened bolt in the chassis, a clapping belt, a bending axle, the slump, wheeze and flap of a deflating tyre.

He slaps the dashboard as if it were the flank of a horse and veers right at a sign saying, *The First Gun Club of B_*.

Four men gather around a small tin hut behind a wooden fence upon which has been nailed a placard declaring with red capitals on white: *THE FIRST GUN CLUB OF B_*.

As Austin approaches with his camera and tripod, Moore Carolan, laughing heartily, turns from the group with his gun barrel broken over his forearm.

'Mr Austin, the great photographer, come forth!' he calls.

Austin shakes Carolan's hand and asks where they might prefer to be photographed.

The four men arrange themselves around the sign in front of the small tin hut; they consist of a retired colonel, wet-eyed and of advanced age, a stout local vet, a young judge who was at one time a leader of an anti-Treaty squadron in the midlands, and then stolid Carolan. They organise themselves into a loose line, then, seemingly unbidden, they stiffen, all of them lifting their chins as Austin, disappearing beneath his black cloth once again and with his left hand raised, indicating a request for motionlessness among his subjects, exposes a plate. Then, he exposes another.

He drops his hand and the men relax. From some fields further behind, a crow caws into the rising whistle of a blackbird. Three of the men step over the fence – two take to the hut and lift a shotgun each, and the third, the aged colonel, saunters over to a mound of yellow ceramic discs heaped upon the black soil twenty yards away.

Carolan approaches Austin with a smile forming on his lips.

'You'll just need the one visit for this, I hope?'

'Just the one,' replies Austin. 'Sorry about all of that.'

'Not a *brón*, we all miss sometimes,' says Carolan, grinning, while looking up at Austin's impassive face.

'Might I have a word someday?' begins Austin, carefully unscrewing the camera from the tripod. 'I've a proposal of sorts, if that would be agreeable?'

'On what?'

'A segment of your land,' says Austin, 'down by the lake and the peninsula off it; do you use it?'

'You mean when it's not flooding?'

'Well, yes.'

'And what sort of thing are you proposing?'

'A golf links, sir.'

Carolan's eyebrows lift in surprise.

He shifts his weight. 'Sure, come and show me what you're considering,' he says, laughing now at the good of it all and the gumption of this young buck.

'I'll call over in the next week, if that's OK?'

'Ring ahead then, Austin; you have my number – Doire Mór, 155.'

2.

Doktor Alois puts a hand out before him and looks at it trembling. Then, he puts out the other, and as he looks at it trembling also, he begins to think that all that is certain about them now is the tremble.

Over the last few days; he has been trying to think about what kinds of things can be said with certainty, but he finds himself stuck in the very foothills of the problem, busying himself with trying to mark out a linguistic terrain where the foundations of what might be said with certainty might be located. This habit of over-preparation is one that has haunted his later life and work, and it stems from a regression to his youth, when his mother used to insist on him and all of his siblings remaking their beds each night before they slept. She would then inspect the tucks and folds before these beds were deemed ready for them to slip into. While Alois is aware of this regression in his work to near-pointless atoms of pedantry, he realises too that he is helpless in counteracting it.

In the last month, the German word for 'layout' has come often to his mind: *Grundriss*. And any time he breaks this word down into *Grund* – ground – and *Riss* – rip, tear – he finds himself nearing a new thought, and into his lined notebook he writes a version of the following sentence: *To tear open the land into which to sit a proposition.* Then he scribbles it out and a day or two later tries yet another formulation, then another, then another. The most recent version is exactly the same as the first, except that he has changed the word 'sit' to 'embed'.

After these recent efforts, he began to picture with some longing the four consecutive summers he spent building this house. He recalled the lengths of timber arriving at his site, short enough to be handleable by one person, yet robust enough to be lengthened end-to-end with metal cleats to produce the sizes and shapes he needed to erect a building in which to live in simple comfort. He regretted the fact that, while he worked with the stone and timber planks, he never took the time, through the actions of his body, to wholly unlearn the assumed meaning, first, of the word 'house' and, by extension, the word 'shelter'. The only thought of any interest that has come to him from his building of this house has been that, while one can hear the structure of the house, especially in wind, one can, he realises, never *hear* the structure of any sentence one might create to describe this sound.

He takes his trembling hands from in front of him and rests them on his lap, and because his thoughts on these and on other such remembrances in recent days have climbed no further, he merely lies back onto his bed, whispering to himself the word *Obdachlos* ('homeless', 'roofless') while he listens out for the creaking of the house around him, before falling into a snooze, or, more precisely, into a semi-consciousness that drops through the trapdoor of a deeper disappearance of his energy, of his will.

Since his first famous early paper, he published only two further pamphlets in Oxford. Both were on linguistic philosophy. One was called *Logic and Faith*, while the other was titled *Faith and Logic*. The first was a short pugnacious treatise told in seven parts. He described it then as having stemmed from the tail end of his time as a logical positivist and in it he continued to insist that the only way philosophy could be taken as seriously as science was if 'all metaphysics was put under the category of nonsense'. He pursued this position to the point in this book where he held that English grammar itself was *suspicious* in how it *cloaked* its logical slovenliness behind the *aura of its use*. Then, eight years later, and just before war broke out, he published the second pamphlet, a more sheepish return to the subject and one that seemed instead to claim that philosophy *ought to unclip itself from the totalising designs of science*. The writing in this book was described by one of his less charitable colleagues in Keble as akin to 'a stricken apostle turning back to the last sun-rays of metaphysics'. The final line of the book was openly mocked, it claiming: *The word 'God' either refers to everything or nothing; it is therefore a nonsense … and yet.*

Alois doesn't think with any clarity about the content of these two works anymore. But often the two resounding images they produced while he wrote them return to mind: the first, a set of seven steps floating in an abyss; the second, a train ride through the Dolomites, while engaged in a sort of Socratic dialogue with a more agitated version of himself about what they can see and then about what they can even claim to see out of the train window as the land and objects pass by. What he is working on now produces two new if incomplete images such as these.

At some of the early sections of this still rather scattered book, he sees in his mind a curly-haired man in his mid-fifties circling a hole, while speaking aloud to himself, but with his hand to his brow. When this man utters sentences using versions of the verb 'to be', he draws nearer to the hole; then, when he utters sentences using versions of all other verbs, this figure draws further away. And when he adds an adverb to these sentences, the hole all but disappears and the sun of the world begins to shine a little brighter and makes the surrounds somewhat warmer. The circling this man makes around the hole is always of an irregular radius, as if the forces of attraction to the hole fluctuate as he at once circumnavigates and *verbs*. The game in his mind, as he writes, is to draw this man as close to the hole as possible while at the same time ensuring he – this entity – never becomes aware or in turn fearful of the hole's existence. Then, during some of the later sections of this scattered new manuscript, the other image that comes to mind consists of this same curly-haired man in his mid-fifties, but now holding a shotgun to his shoulder, on the cusp of calling, 'Pull!' When he does so, some unseen figure to his left hurls with a mechanical sling a yellow disk, a clay pigeon, high into the air, and the man, upon shooting, either obliterates this clay pigeon mid-air, or misses and both pellet-cluster and clay pigeon criss-cross and soar down to the turf, hundreds of yards away from each other. Alois imagines the ground as a vast open bog, not so wet as to be swamp and not so dry as to be harvestable; and he imagines the sky above this to be grey-brown and low, and perpetually on the cusp of rain. He imagines, then, whenever the marksman obliterates a clay pigeon, that he silently advances to the point in the bog where the disintegrated clay pigeon has rained down and, in the circle of tiny yellow fragments, he stands, puts his shotgun to his shoulder once more and calls out another 'Pull!' – to which another clay pigeon silently arcs into the air, ascending to destruction or descending to stillness. Alois considers each of these successful gunshots as a paragraph he has written that has pleased him or that has advanced him a step or two towards the lands in which a suitable terrain might be marked out to attempt to say something with certainty.

He rises from his bed once more and sits on his chair. He opens out his notebook and realises that his handwriting has deteriorated so badly it is now illegible even to him. He flips back some pages to see where his handwriting was last legible. He reads over these lines with a look of disgust forming on his face.

He closes the notebook, then he turns to the corner of his room where the child's kite now lies.

I.

Moore Carolan sits back in his armchair in the stone-floored kitchen of his farmhouse. The door behind swings over and back, and in through it drifts the clank and call of men harvesting in the fields.

Carolan doesn't farm the land himself, but instead employs agents and seasonal farmhands to carry out the work. Sometimes, he saddles up his horse, a white mare called Milly, and takes her out into the fields at the end of the day to inspect the wherewithal of the place. Most times, while on these slow walks, he thinks about the foreign-currency betting he has undertaken of late. He has made thousands in recent months, more than he has ever made before, and yet he does not want to cash his earnings in, on account of the competitiveness he feels with his older brother, Gilbert, now ensconced in his usual front room, in his usual small stone guest house, in St Peter Port in Guernsey. Carolan has been reading the latest articles by 'that great mind' Keynes in *The Manchester Guardian*, where he makes it clear that the British and European currencies are due to fall further while the dollar is only to grow more mighty. Carolan, sitting in his kitchen, listening now to the distant clink of a plough being uncoupled from a horse, is considering putting almost all of what he has earned into US dollars with a view to claiming, some weeks down the line, the great excess squeezed out of the growth of this seemingly magical currency. Then, he has promised himself that he will purchase a second house and farm, put the remainder in low-risk shares and cease this currency betting forever.

He goes to the phone at the hallway window that looks over his small manicured lawn of shrubs and bright wavering flowers, with a white bench along a stone wall that he and his brother built a decade ago to mark out where farm ends and home begins. He asks the operator to put him through to his broker in London and he instructs this broker to buy ten thousand pounds' worth of US dollars. Then, he returns to the kitchen, lights a cigarette and, as he takes his first draw, Catherine wanders in from school. She places her satchel onto the kitchen table and wordlessly puts her arms around her father's neck, and there they sit and stand awhile, he looking at the smoke spiralling from the tip of his cigarette, she looking askance at a picture of the Holy Mother of Christ, her arms wide, palms outward, all of her aglow above the calendar month of May. Looking at the arrangement of angels around the Virgin Mother, Catherine sums the dates of the month from one to thirty-one; then, holding this sum in mind, she begins to divide it by each number, descending from thirty-one, holding the result and remainders in a pocket in her mind that has only recently popped into existence. The numbers in this pocket she adds together and she begins to divide this total by each date on the calendar, but this time moving from one up to thirty-one. Then, becoming listless at the increasing ease of this game, she looks once more at the Virgin Mother, her large blue eyes gazing back at Catherine, and to this Catherine feels her father pat her head and make to rise.

Austin, in his darkroom across the county – while under a red light dully illuminating sheets of paper showing the four inaugural members of the First Gun Club of B_ – ruminates over his encounter with Clare. He thinks for a moment about that fair ringlet of hair around her ear, framing the gorgeous swerves and contours shining and shadowing in the ear-slung light. He lifts a sheet of photographic paper from the tray of lilting water, holds it a moment, then he clips it to a red nylon line above his head. He looks at the emerging image awhile longer, taking in the sharpening features of these men's faces and bodies, and the dark folds of land beyond. He notes that Moore Carolan is not looking into the camera in this photograph, nor in the second one. In both, he is looking over Austin's shoulder at something far off behind. Austin reckons that nonetheless both photographs will be fit for posting to the newspaper later in the day, for publication in the Local Notes of next week's edition. Then Austin hopes to spend the rest of this week formalising his golf-course layouts with the aim of arranging a meeting with Carolan about this project on his land.

Stepping from his darkroom, Austin takes his cup of cold black tea from his table. As often happens in these quieter moments, he recalls that day almost two years ago when his mother entered his cottage and told him to leave the county before his father returned home. She said that she had learned about him selling 'for mere blasted money' the locations of explosives stores belonging to the small anti-Treaty militant group of which his younger brother was a member. She told him with an anger that shook her voice that his own brother was maimed and near close to death from an attack there last night and that his father was returning to exact revenge … 'You had best go, boy,' she said quietly to Austin, and to this he stood and left his abode forever.

Taking a sip from his tea, he bends his head as he steps through the rough doorway to the next room, and he advances to his drawing table. Across the table's surface drapes the large drawing of 'The Elms', his signature eighteenth hole.

Austin stands by the drawing, gazing on at the row of elm trees he has indicated along the fairway; they follow the shape of those – as he remembers them – leading up to his mother's house. He takes in, too, how the putting green he has fashioned into the gun-shaped outline of the county of Roscommon protrudes gently into the lake. He imagines water lapping peacefully at the foot of this green, where stone and reed turns to pebble, then loam, then grass. He imagines men turning from this putting green and admiring the bucolic undulations of this flag-dotted land as it runs up to the dark forest. He lifts a clutch pencil and indicates a phantom contour line, then another, then another, in gentle swerves and swirls. He lifts a scrap of tracing paper and onto it he indicates the tee box and the furthest edge of the eighteenth green, 415 yards away, and while looking at these contours, on the other drawing he marks out a cross-section of the entire hole, showing how it dips and how it rises along the fairway and up to the putting green with a hole in the middle from which a flag protrudes seven feet above the surface. He takes a red pencil and colours in the flag; then, with a blue pencil, he indicates a hint of summer sky. As he steps back and takes in this whole cross-section, it occurs to him that this will be the second set of eighteen drawings he will bring with him to Moore Carolan; he reckons the topographical clarity of these cross-sections will surely show his seriousness, aid his case, and perhaps enthuse his wealthy would-be patron.

2.

After a wet morning, Alois and Catherine decide to take lunch outside in the afternoon sun. It's blowy and the white tablecloth that Alois insisted on draping over the table flaps at its corners and is threatening at any moment to overturn itself.

Together, they had set the table for a three-course meal of soup, steak and a dessert of trifle – a recipe that Catherine's mother gave to her the morning she first left London for St Hugh's.

Sitting at right angles to each other, Alois pops his last bottle of Riesling, one from his family's vineyard. It was bottled in late 1928, a few months before he left Kaltern forever. His sister Ines sent it after the war, with another bottle of *a lovely late-summer grape* and a note pleading him to visit. He wrote back saying that he would come *some Christmas soon*, but he never fulfilled this promise. He struggled to square the ease with which his family – and his father's wine company – had joined the ranks of the fascists and stayed loyal to the regime for years, even helping to fund a monstrous 'Monument to Victory' in Bolzano, just over the town's main river bridge, at that junction between the old town and what they now call 'the new town'. His sisters claimed it was necessary for their business to exist, to thrive, but Alois was suspicious of the speed with which his father had shifted sides and he was sure it was not all just some show of pragmatism, but was a kind of 'weather-cock convenience' that revealed a void in the family's make-up where Alois felt principle should have stood, and this suspicion grew and grew in him, unshackled through his distance from his family, into a feeling of disgust – one he, however, has never elucidated aloud.

He sniffs the underside of the cork and then pours two glasses.

After their first two courses, Catherine returns to the table, having cleared it of its plates.

Alois, with a toothpick between his fingers, looks to Catherine with a platonic admiration as the breeze plays with her dark hair, and he asks her if she would like another glass of this 'last of the Kaltern wine', to which she nods while pushing to one side of the table her packet of cigarettes.

'A grand day now,' she says, squinting into the sun as a seagull overhead screams.

She lifts her wine glass to her nose before taking a sip. Alois meanwhile thrusts his narrow nose into the glass and breathes deeply, then quaffs back a great mouthful of this cool yellow Riesling.

'The old fascist could make wine, at least,' he says, looking down into the glass as he swirls it expertly, before taking another gulp.

Then he coughs and coughs again, then is silent until he begins to cough some more, but with increasing weakness, for almost half a minute. Catherine, out of a sort of polite denial, looks off towards the dunes. A local fisherman spins past on his bicycle and waves at them both, and Catherine waves in return. 'A lovely day for fishing?'

'We'll see!' comes the reply.

Alois, wheezing now, grasps the two arms of his chair as he tries to draw full breath. Then his body, all sinew, relents and he sits there, puce of face, like a chastened boy.

Catherine places her hand onto his bony knee and holds it for a while, until Alois takes her hand in his.

'I'm sorry, C.,' he says, without looking up. 'I'm so sorry we didn't spend more time together when we could ...'

Catherine looks away, as if following the fisherman's wobbling progress.

'Well, we still have all of now,' she replies, looking to Alois.

She lifts her hand from his and puts her knuckles gently to his face awhile. A tear forms in his eye.

She then stands and makes for the kitchen to bring the trifles out.

Alois looks skyward at the same wheeling seagull soaring over and back, and to this he closes his eyes for some moments.

At the front porch, Catherine reappears bearing a patterned bowl of trifle in each hand. She sits and they eat the sweet in an easy silence. Catherine has come to enjoy their easy silences – she knows it is what she will miss most – and she enjoys, too, when Alois calls her 'C.'

Then, Alois turns to her and says, 'I'd no idea they'd asked you to take part at Bomber Command during the war.'

Catherine spoons some trifle into her mouth, savours it and then returns her gaze to Alois.

'And who told you about that?' she asks.

'A young chap I met while visiting Sraffa in Cambridge some years ago. He was called Dyson. A tall man, limpid grey eyes, brainy.'

'Well, I was invited, if that's what you mean. I think it was for the work I was doing on probability at the time,' says Catherine, peering at her bloated reflection in the spoon. 'They were surprised to hear of someone revisiting Bayes' work and mapping his dimensions of probability onto the dimensions of space. My project all led to nothing, really, Alois – it barely went beyond speculation – but you can imagine why they, in their world of ballistics and out of some desperation, might have thought that I could be of use.'

'And were you not curious to see their offices, their workshops?' asks Alois, placing with a dull tinkle his spoon back into his bowl.

Catherine looks into Alois's eyes, trying to guess where he is going with this and how much he wants to eke from her about her feelings ... what he wants her to say.

'I thought it was a barbaric place.' She smiles. 'You know all about the firestorms they made in Dresden, in Hamburg? You know how they measured out that destruction. That is evil, also, no?'

'It was a thorough carrying-out of a bureaucracy, Catherine ... I'm not arguing with that ... but you could not have known that then. Now, please tell me, why did you not go? You could have been of use … It would have greatly helped your career, your reputation afterwards – *in with all of the clever boys*, as it were.'

'Was I not of use in Guy's?' she asks. 'You know I could not have helped at St Hugh's … the head-injury nurses were too specialised to need me there; so, Guy's seemed obvious, no?'

'I'm not joking, Catherine.'

At this, she looks away.

'I'm glad I went to Guy's,' she says, almost to herself; then she peers into her bowl. 'Otherwise, I'd never have got to know you.'

Alois puts the trifle dish onto the table and he looks at Catherine until she once again turns away.

She can tell in this kind of silence that he will say something hurtful now.

'You are a fool,' he says.

'I know,' she replies, without turning back, 'but I wish I was far more foolish.'

'You know I could never have …'

She nods, still looking away.

Then, with a gust of wind, the table rattles, and Catherine, knuckling her eye, reaches out to take her glass of Riesling, which she sips and sips again until its end.

Then she carefully lights a cigarette.

I.

In her bedroom, young Catherine Carolan sits at a small desk by her window.

Cattle low outside as she opens a small copybook and begins to write a series of letters, from memory, of a stanza she glimpsed for mere moments earlier that day while she stood beside Master Francis, who was looking through her copybook at a set of sums. She begins with a shaky letter *A*, then below it:

s
s
o
m
e
f
a
i
r
f
e

m
a
l
e
unadornedandplain
s
e
c
u
r
e
t
o
p
l
e
a
s
e
whileyouthconfirmsherreign
s
l
i
g
h
t
s
e
v

e
r
y
b
o
r
r
o
w
e
d
c
h
a
r
m
thatdresssupplies
n
o
r
s
h
a
r
e
s
withartthetriumphofhereyes

2.

In late afternoon, in the kitchen of *Haus Alois*, and with all of the plates and cutlery stacked onto the table, Catherine and Alois stand, holding each other in what, if they were moving at all, might be called a slow dance.

If it were possible to hear what Alois hears, we would hear Catherine gently tra-la-la-ing into his ear the alto line of a song a churchgoer would recognise as 'Abide with Me'.

1.

Young Catherine's mother steps quietly into her daughter's bedroom and, peering over Catherine's shoulder at this list of random-seeming letters she is writing out, at once so mechanically and so full of intention, she asks, 'What are you up to now, dear?'

Catherine looks back over her shoulder and replies to her mother, 'Doing letters.'

'To whom?' asks Elizabeth.

'Oh, nobody!' replies Catherine.

2.

Outside, the land and sea have grown dark.

Catherine helps a leaden Alois up to his bed, where she lays him down, easing his head onto a pillow.

She makes to leave, but he puts out a hand as if to show her that he would like her to take it. She places her hand into his.

That night, after the dishes are washed and put away, and after the house has fallen quiet, Catherine takes her navy notebook out and carefully writes the following:

If I assume that at least two persons exist, then:
If
$\forall x\ \exists y[L(x,y)]$
Everybody loves someone.

Then
$\exists x\ \exists y\ [L(x,y)]$
There exists some x, there exists some y, such that x is in love with y.

Or

$\exists y \, \exists x \, [L(y,x)]$

There exists some y, there exists some x, such that y is in love with x.

But if

x = Catherine

y = Alois

Then

$L(x,y) \nvDash L(y,x)$

x loves y does not entail that y loves x.

I.

Young Catherine turns from her mother and looks back over her list of letters. Then she continues to carefully pencil more of them in, one after the other, on each successive line, before moving horizontally with another burst of poorly formed and cramped glyphs.

'May I see your letters?' asks Elizabeth.

And Catherine hands her notebook up to her mother, but so poor is her penmanship and so without punctuation or spacings is the writing, that her mother fails to recognise the language in it all and merely smiles and returns the copybook to Catherine's outstretched hands. Elizabeth then looks out the window at the clouds lifting east and suggests to Catherine that she go to the chicken coop and check for an egg.

Catherine silently returns once more to her copybook and begins to pencil the rest of those letters she saw for that moment by Master Francis's side, as if by doing so she will vent some urge to express this crystallising capacity, this sheer excess, of memory. Her mother steps to Catherine's desk and gently pulls the copybook from underneath her pencil, and as Catherine looks up, her mother smiles and asks her if she has already forgotten about the chicken coop and the egg.

'You love the little chickens, no?' she says.

Catherine leaves for the coop as her mother has asked, but this urge to play with this capacity of memory will only grow more fierce through her life and it will find her favourite form of expression by her third year of study in St Hugh's, where she will develop a method for making lecture notes whereby she will sit, somewhat disconcertingly, in front of the lecturer, and over the course of the three-hour lecture will look almost without blinking at the person delivering this information, never writing so much as a word into her notebook, but instead scanning the rotating blackboards as the teachings are relayed, and then, over the course of a mere ten minutes after each lecture, Catherine, in the empty hall, will lift her pencil and reproduce the lecture in the form of the underlying structure with which the lecturer had delivered it, showing the salient moments of *new information* at each node of the network that Catherine casts out across her notebook pages.

On one occasion, a senior tutor called Maud Wrinch will approach Catherine as she completes a set of such notes, and she will ask Catherine if she finds these lectures tedious at all.

'You just sit there, staring, Catherine,' Maud will say politely, inquisitively.

'Oh, I find them fascinating, though,' Catherine will reply. 'They're like scaffolding for a new thought, I think. And I learn from this, too, Dr Wrinch, the shape of each lecturer's thoughts, and how they organise what it is they hope to say to us. That's really what fascinates me … these things,' Catherine will say, gesturing at her notebook with her pencil. 'All of my notes then just become a lens into the nature of the lecturer and their *manner of knowledge*, rather than, say, a frame for looking through … and the reason I prefer a lens over a frame, Dr Wrinch, is because a lens brings with it playful distortions that a frame never can … and I enjoy trying to handle these distortions, if you see what I mean …'

2.

It is some days after their outdoor meal, and Catherine, in a series of sharp draws, finishes her cigarette, stubbing it into a pink ceramic bowl with pastoral images of alpine mountains on its side. It was found by Alois in a flea market in central Oxford one quiet Sunday after Easter five years ago.

Catherine leaves the kitchen table and brings the ashtray to the window ledge, where she then opens out the window.

She and Alois agreed after their dinner that, on the next fine day when he feels up to it, they should take some air along the sea. He said to her this morning that he was, once more, feeling 'robust'.

He calls to her from the top of the stairs and she goes to him, leading him down, his free hand grasping and ungrasping the maple banister as he descends – a banister he planed and polished for a whole week some fifteen years before.

A few days previously he had given Catherine a tour of the house, describing how he had constructed it. She'd asked about the two posts holding the stairwell and the upper floor in place. She'd called these posts 'macabre', and to this he laughed. They were of stained wood, stout, but carved in such a way that along their length emerged points like small beaks of trapped birds trying to pierce the skin of the thing from within. He said he'd bought two electricity poles from the timber merchant who had provided all of the timber for the rest of the house – broad planks of cypress grown near to slow inland rivers. Alois said that these poles had been rough when they arrived and, as he began to plane and smoothen them, he realised that there were some knots not worth trying to remove, so instead he improvised around them, down the length of the poles; thus these beak-like points. 'I love them,' he said, running his hand over a beak, and to this Catherine merely looked them up and down. Then, he walked her to the fireplace and the chimney flue above, of which he told her he was especially proud. 'It provides the stability for the whole building,' he said, clapping his palm against its surface, rough with oversized aggregate and concrete. 'I cast it in seven pieces, each decreasing in size up to the chimney pot,' he said. He told her that he'd wanted to reproduce in this chimney piece the clastic patterning of a strange limestone that appears in the land north of Bolzano. 'It's called Höttinger Brekzie,' he said. 'Gorgeous pale and sometimes red stone, and when you burn this house down for me,' he continued, 'this single stalagmite of stone is all that will remain.'

'Burn down?' she asked.

'Yes, to the ground,' he replied.

At this, Catherine frowned. 'I'll not burn down anything, Alois,' she said.

'You must,' he replied, stepping to her, 'and my body shall be in it, too.'

To this, she merely looked at him, and as the house creaked around them once more in a gust of passing wind, their eyes met, and lingered – more than lingered: rested. They stood there for some time, until Alois put out his hand and Catherine gently took it.

'I'm glad we are agreed,' he then said, and at this she dropped her hand from his and they stepped apart.

'Please come,' he said, and he left for his room upstairs, where he showed her the two models he'd made of his house: one in a state of completeness, shining in a shaft of afternoon sun, the other singed and darkened. He presented to her a drawing to the right of the burned-down model, showing the plan of the ground floor; criss-crossing it were red lines, and to these Alois pointed and said, 'There's a jerrycan full of gasoline beneath the stairs. On the morning after I pass, use this gasoline to draw out these lines across my house and then, when you have said your farewells, as it were, please use the matches on my table there to set the place alight.'

Catherine looked at him, her lower lip trembling. She shook her head slowly, while knuckling a tear from her eye, and she then silently made her way downstairs.

Out on the strand, the sunlight slips through from between two clouds. Catherine tells Alois that today is April first and, to help lift his spirits, she asks if there are any old April fools' jokes he can recall from his youth.

He falls silent, pursing his lips, his hair blowing around his crown, while taking this frivolous question in that over-serious way she has come to love. Then he begins to tell her about the joke his older sister, Ines, once played on him when he was eight, when she sat him down on their parents' bed and told him that there was no such thing as God.

'It was only days after my first communion, you know,' he says, smiling. 'I remember sitting there dumbly, on the edge of tears, but she insisted, "No, no, my dear Josef," she said. "No Christ, no Holy Spirit, no Virgin Mother ... All made up," she said.'

Catherine takes his arm as they walk along the stiff wet sand, the sun coming and going now, sparkling and dulling the crashing surf.

'It was a good joke, you know,' he says, smiling, as he wipes a wind-whipped wetness from his eyes. 'I haven't believed in any of that nonsense since!'

'And where is Ines now?' asks Catherine, pushing with her fingers strands of her blowing black hair from her cheek.

'Oh, I've not spoken to any of them for years.'

'But do they know of the turn you've taken?'

'I'll not trouble them with any of this shit, Catherine. I can tell 'em all when I see them next. It'll be something for us to talk about, at least ... It might be funny, when I see them in the next world, having something of interest at last to tell them, but no words with which to relay it ... We can all sit together forever, C., looking at each other, mute, in that ghostly silence of heavenly speech!'

Alois begins to slow, and with this Catherine releases his hand and they turn. He stalls awhile, wincing, looking up sometimes at Catherine, sometimes out helplessly to sea.

‘Damnation is where we are, Catherine,’ he pants, taking her arm. ‘Damnation … I am so sorry for bringing you here, and yet I am so glad you are here.’

He leans down, puts his hands onto his knees and heaves for breath for almost a minute. Catherine stands back, not wholly sure if yet to intervene. Then she gently places her hands around his flanks, as if he were a wounded foal.

A woman appears at the far end of the strand, her blond hair a fright of white in the breeze. She puts a hand to her eyes and peers at these two distant figures until the one bent over straightens and leans into the young dark-haired woman whose red cotton dress distorts against the wind. The woman at the far end of the strand turns away when she realises this distant couple are now engaged in an embrace. Had she kept looking at this couple of concern, however, she would have seen that the embrace was Catherine catching Alois in a shaking hold before he slumped to the ground.

Hanging from her there, his eyes now swimming in their sockets, his face drained of colour and in a grimace, and with his tiny heart pounding, Alois whispers, ‘Catherine, what is the meaning of this?’

I.

Austin, who rarely drinks when driving his automobile, is sitting in the front seat drinking from a small bottle of whiskey. Through the dark, he can make out the angled roof edges and windows of the Dean Russell dance hall in the distance, from which vibrant music pours. He leans forward and peers at the men and women leaving and arriving amid a great trill of laughter and the thrum of a gay new melody coming to life.

Not twenty minutes before, he had walked across the dance-hall floor to ask Clare Dargan for a dance, and she, sitting with some friends, at first hesitated, and then looked up at him, took his hand and they partook in a rather frigid-seeming jig. When the dance came to an end, she thanked him politely, but did not linger for a second more, and once she took her seat among her friends, all girls half a decade younger than her, she began to gaze alluringly, Austin felt, across the bright dance-hall floor at Master Francis, who was there with the eldest son of the headmaster. A rowdy reel then filled the hall from the whistles, strings, hands and feet of the four aged and perspiring musicians on the stage.

Master Francis looked over his shoulder at Clare, who was smiling through the music and chatter back at him. He put his glass of lemon cordial down on the circular table around which the men had gathered and he walked across the dance floor to Clare, who was on her feet before he arrived. It was with a dull ache in his stomach that Austin watched Clare and Master Francis happily and naturally and at times beautifully dance not one, but two and three dances in a row. It was midway through the third dance that Austin cast a forlorn look around the dance hall and left.

He ignites the engine of his Model T and cranks it into gear. As he moves off, he imagines Clare sitting there beside him, them both heading into the dark of the countryside, each breathless at the enclosed proximity of the other. He imagines, as they go, she gently placing her hand onto his knee. He puts the whiskey aside and drives with care back to his fourth-floor rooms, lies on his bed, closes his eyes and, with some ease, relieves himself, and with a flannel then cleans his belly of the oily white dollops shaken so brilliantly from himself not seconds before; then, he falls asleep.

He wakes at dawn and, in the blue morning light, he stands at his drawing board and completes the cross-sectional drawings depicting the rises and falls of the last four layouts of his golf course. He rolls all of the drawings up and around them affixes a cardboard sleeve, upon which he writes in black capitals the words *FAO Moore Carolan*, and he places the roll onto his kitchen table.

Then he lifts a folder full of family portraits he's recently taken and, while flicking through these well-composed photographs, he decides that he will try, so as to expand his business, to add colour-tinting to his next suite. To warm them up a little, he thinks. Then, he places the folder onto his workbench, pulls on his blazer and makes to leave.

He is to play in another Ferns Cup game later today, this time at the old Royal Oaks Golf Club, a new course about twenty miles west of B_.

He steps from his brightening fourth-floor lodgings, not knowing that he will never return.

2.

Catherine Carolan leans over to dab at Alois's brow and his gaunt cheeks, all the while whispering, 'There, there, Josef. There, there.'

They had been talking for some time through the early afternoon – she on his chair, he at first reclined then fully lying back on his bed – about integers and whole numbers. They were discussing the idea of numbers as objects that can not only count objects, but also count themselves. There are nine moons around Saturn, while also nine prime numbers between and including the numbers two and twenty-three. This, they agreed, made a number such a strange sort of object in the world, but objects, Alois always contended, that were not in the 'causal nexus' – they were not part of the link between cause and effect . . . 'You can't knock something over with a number,' he said. Catherine could never usually, and could not on this occasion either, agree with this, 'Tempting but erroneous, Alois!' she replied, smiling. She always felt that there was something in numbers that did touch the world of causation, and she had held on to this flicker of a thought with a strange firmness, all the more realised one morning, some months later, when she read at last the Englishman Turing's paper *On Computational Numbers* and she realised that numbers were far more than mere objects, but were also machines. Alois had warned her through the years they knew each other of these *ontological leaps* she was prone to making between different categories of things, and this warning came to mind that morning too, some months later, in the quiet of her room in St Hugh's, as she pushed this new idea to one side.

Alois, lying there, slips into a snooze, so Catherine sits back and places her damp cloth onto the table. Then she pulls her chair close to his bed and takes Alois's limp hand in hers and she strokes it awhile.

Alois then, through closed eyes and smiling slyly, utters, 'Do you think, C., will I only become a complete object in that moment before I go? And, if so, do you think this completeness will only occur upon my last inhalation? Or will this completeness arrive only at my exhalation?'

Then, with his breathing becoming more laboured, he whispers as if from somewhere far beyond this room, 'I remember, C., the day a lecturer in Bolzano told me, when I was young, that a weir, when placed into a river, not only affects the water downstream, as you would expect, but also far upstream too. Isn't that so queer? I still think it is …'

After a few moments of a gusting wind rising and passing outside, Catherine stands and places her hand upon Alois's cheek.

He, lying there silently and motionless, remembers, as his mind fades to darkness again, the sound of an old oil press his father made in the basement of their first home on the southern hills between Kaltern and Kaltern See. The house would shake whenever the blindfolded donkey below turned the giant grindstone around its vertical axle, and with the sound of this turning in mind Alois then pictures the first day they opened the cable car up to the Mendel Pass on the hill at the top of Kaltern town, and his mother, on that day they took their first cable-car trip up into the hills, grasping his young hand as they surged over a cloud-enshrouded support. He realises now as he falls asleep that her taking his hand was probably not so much to comfort him as to settle her too.

Catherine lingers by Alois awhile, then she goes to his table and opens his lined notebook and tries to make sense of the most recent pages of notes he's made. With some effort, he seems to have re-erected his writing in these last few days into legibility, and she reads in his strangely stilted German prose:

Putting the height of my house in relation to, say, a church steeple, the height of interruption of the sky is then low. This house, or at least dwellings of this domestic kind, break the sky at a distance that is almost touchable to a mortal. This house was within the scale of me as I built it, as I habituated it, and it will come closer to me still when I destroy it.

If a man of six feet tall extended his arm and reached up, he could touch the underside of the gutter of my house, which is the place where the roof extends up towards its apex – where the house begins and where it begins to cease to be.

If we draw, then, two arcs up to the apex of the roof, we are still within the realm of the Earth and the mortal. And if we extend these crossing arcs past each other and out into the unmeasurable, the unknown, we can take these extensions now only to be a function of the earth and the mortal. But when they are extended beyond the apex – this point of collision and destruction – these arcs then become the unknowable sky and the divine.

I.

Austin, after winning his evening golf match four and three – a sliding downhill putt on the fifteenth green – decided to take a few drinks in the clubhouse with some of his more ribald, older teammates. A clutch of these corpulent middle-aged men – a solicitor, a short-sighted senior civil servant, a recently retired doctor – stayed till late, discussing who their next opponent might be. They agreed that, if the club is by the coast, then they'd all have to practise a flattening out of their swings for the inevitable sea winds.

Austin, enlivened by all of this, was one of the last to leave. He is now driving at speed across the dark countryside towards his boarding house in B_. Amid the rattles and shunts, he leans forward to listen out for a growing thump emerging from the chassis. He rides a hill as if it were a wave, the wheels stretching to touch the ground. Then, he feels the shaft of the steering wheel fall horribly slack and, in the next moment, as he twists the steering wheel this way and that, the road beneath him disappears and he feels as if this wagon has taken full flight, which it has, past a raised turn before a canal bridge. His Model T, revving wildly, crashes into the black water below, knocking Austin immediately into semi-consciousness, shattered glass spraying hither and thither; the car slows, then turns over in the reed-lined water. The roof of the car drifts down and meets the stony floor of the canal. As water courses down Austin's opened throat, his foot hits the accelerator, revving the engine violently until it floods and splutters out.

Then, a lapping silence. A distant corncrake's call.

Through the dark, a light comes on in the lock-master's house, which sits at the next turn in the canal, half a mile away. Inside, the old man is firing up a small stagecoach lantern so as to step out into the cold and investigate this sudden racket beyond.

For a moment, in the upturned car, Austin regains a grasp of this world, and what comes to mind is not his beloved Clare Dargan, nor his mother, his maimed and murdered brother, his estranged father, but instead he sees for the briefest moment, and for a reason he will never fathom, the X that the young Carolan girl made with her arms outside a house between a shining forest and a set of fields that run down to a lake ensconced in a handsome corner of agrarian land, full of potential, on the other side of the county.

2.

Alois is lying on his bed, barely breathing.

It is now evening and Catherine is sitting alone downstairs, her chin propped in her hand, and looking out the window at a deep sea mist rolling in and slowly enveloping the land, the distant view of Aberdeen, the row of bungalows and then, too, this house. Catherine imagines this mist transforming into a giant hand reaching for the building, and the small creaks upstairs she, for a moment, attributes to the stealthy fingers of this hand finally taking its grasp. The sea outside seems also to disappear, and with it the sound of the waves lapping weakly.

The light then begins to fall too, until everything outside the house seems to cease in its material existence. Catherine wonders, if some entity were looking on at this house from beyond, would this house and all of its inhabitants – she and Alois – cease to exist to this onlooking figure, too?

Then, from the edge of the window frame, the distant Belt Ness lighthouse lamp traces out a vague beam of lemon through it all. Then, even this light disappears.

The sea waves have frozen over and, to this, Alois, upstairs, rises from his bed and stands at the window for a while. He has forgotten that Catherine is downstairs. He thinks he is wholly alone, looking into this shifting grey vapour, until, after almost half an hour of this vacant looking, a break appears and from it a shred of the world, a quadrilateral of light from a neighbouring bungalow, then the dunes, the strand, the waves, a distant if luminous bobbing red buoy, and the surprised screech of a bird, as if she has just awoken to a row of stranger's eggs secreted beneath her in the dark, the alien blue sheen of their shells now coming up in the pale sunlight of another planet's dawn.

1.

Master Francis, sitting at the top of his quiet classroom, turns over in his mind the news he received from Clare this morning about the crash on the outskirts of B_. He recalls seeing some of that awkwardly mannered photographer's reproductions in the local newspaper each week – all clear images of well-composed lines of men with their chins in the air. He pictures Austin's long figure for a moment, crumpled upside down in a car, his slackened mouth breathing in gallons of dank canal water.

Master Francis stands before his class of eleven students, all of them dutifully writing out lines of prayer for inspection after break. He thinks back to the evening of dancing with Clare, the close quarters, the hand-touching walk in the tree-lined night, a hurried inconsequential kiss, the rush of the breeze while bicycling away. He thinks about the moment in all of this when the excitement of acting out some tradition – asking a girl to dance and her acquiescing – fell away into dread at her open-mouthed proximity, and then his sudden and total lack of interest.

He can hear the local curate Father Wall next door, leaving the headmaster's schoolroom. Both men are now laughing heartily over some footballing rivalry, Francis discerns, played out the weekend before on some patch of delineated field to the north of the county.

Then, without knocking, this jovial Father Wall enters the classroom and approaches Master Francis while smiling at the children, who all stand and call out their almost industrialised Gaelic greeting: '*Dia dhuit a Áthair!*'

Master Francis shakes Father Wall's hand and says to him, a mere but sincere, 'Welcome, Father.'

'And how are the children behaving? How are they learning?' asks Father Wall, turning to the class with a giant smile across his broad and bearded face.

'All excellently,' says Master Francis. 'They are a formidable bunch!'

'*An-mhaith!*' says the priest, his soft unworked hands now meeting at the fingertips. 'I won't stay long, but I've a question I'd like to put to the class, and the winner will be awarded a leather-bound missal at the end of term.'

Then, he turns with a whisk of his black vestment to Master Francis and asks, 'Have they been learning their counties and county towns? And do they know much about our dreadful neighbours – those of the *United Kingdom*, as it were?'

Master Francis points to a wall map of the two craggy land masses off the edge of Europe, showing Ireland and England, Scotland and Wales. While alongside it hangs a much larger, newer and more colourful map showing the abstracted sea-less island of Ireland, its four provinces, the counties and their thirty-two county towns.

The priest then wonders aloud, while theatrically stroking his beard, 'Tell me now, children, after Belfast, what is the closest city to Dublin?'

He points the city of Dublin out on the map.

Then, both he and Master Francis peer down at the children, all of whose eyes move to the map of Ireland on the wall. They study it awhile, with scrunched-up faces.

A young, bright and able boy, John Quinn – the sole son of the Quinns, tillage farmers, new to the county and who work the land that runs up to the rear wall of the schoolhouse – raises a hand. Father Wall gestures for him to speak.

'Galway, Father,' he says, with a degree of certainty.

'No,' says Father Wall, looking around at the remaining students. 'Please, try again!'

The children's faces frown in puzzlement once more as they study the map of Ireland.

'Limerick' is offered, then another child calls, 'Cork! Derry!' Then, in gormless desperation, 'Kilkenny!' It is 'scarcely a city at all', they are told.

'Waterford?' is then said, in weak incredulity.

'Bah! Sure, that's only a town!' replies Father Wall, smiling.

Silence.

Some birds call outside as a breeze topples blossoms from the eaves. They cascade like snow to the ground below, and before Father Wall, awkward in the growing quiet, makes to leave, Master Francis, looking to Catherine Carolan staring quietly over and back between the maps on the wall, asks, 'And what do you think there, little Catherine?'

She turns from the maps, her dark eyes looking into him in that strange way he has noted of late, as if her thoughts only finished formulating some moments after he spoke to her, as if she inhabits a time beyond him and from which he merely calls her back, and she whispers, out of timidity in the presence of the broad-shouldered priest, 'The second-closest city is not in Ireland.'

But, because she does not know how to pronounce 'Liverpool', she rises instead and walks to the map of the British Isles, and she points to the large black dot beside the word *Liverpool*. She looks to Master Francis, and then to this large and cheerful priest.

'Now, there's a little thinker,' says Father Wall, as he steps towards her and rubs her head, he like a giant beside her, as she peers up at his dark foreboding bulk.

Then, he turns to Master Francis, shakes his hand and bids them all farewell. At the door, he turns back a moment with an almost carnival-like arch of his torso and says, 'You know, I've been to ten schools in the parish and not one child got even near to the answer … I'll be back with the missal, soon, so!' And, with that, he leaves.

The school handbell ding-dongs next door.

Master Francis takes a cigarette from his packet and tells the children to go out and sport. They rummage for their packed plain sandwiches and, with screeching and banging, they run off out into the back field and begin to cavort in that chaotic first rush that always soon settles into pockets of age-oriented order, then disorder again, before some vague pattern of improvised play takes form once more.

Master Francis lights his cigarette and, out of curiosity, he takes the long wooden ruler from the foot of the blackboard and, at the old map of the British Isles, he places one end of the ruler at Dublin and lines the edge of the ruler up with Liverpool. He makes a delicate white mark on the wood, then he rotates the ruler slightly to line up with the city of Manchester and notes that it lies about one fifth further away. Then he swings the ruler 180 degrees around to Galway and sees it is about the same distance from Dublin as Manchester. He stands back from the map and tries to see if this is obvious at first glance and he thinks to himself, 'No, that's not all that obvious at all.'

2.

The day after the evening of mist, a deeper syncopated quiet falls over *Haus Alois*.

Catherine and Alois barely budge, subdued seemingly by the sounds of the rain tumbling gently outside. In this quiet, Catherine sets to work in her green notebook, refining and at times rebuilding this outline structure for her set of ten lectures and tutorials, designed for her new intake of third-year philosophy undergraduates at St Hugh's, where she will present these strange new 'ideas on phenomenology' she has come to admire. She has since decided to structure the lectures not in relation to the mathematical models she thought interesting at first, but instead on the subject of animal perception, and to present to the students first these other ways of 'being in the world', while taking into account the perspectives and the bodies of 'animals', 'madmen', 'primitives', and to propose a method for finding a logic that might underpin and model these other worlds of reason – *like a logic of plants, or colour*, she notes. She wonders what form the logic might take as it is lifted, dripping, from these other worlds. Her hope, in doing all of this, is that the students might elevate themselves beyond the ambit, the structures, of those she has learned from, and that she might offer her students not so much facts and an order of events and developments, but a method for seeing, a practical wisdom, even, for each student in her care to develop and in turn surge beyond her and what she can hope to give. Sometimes her thoughts circle in great backward arcs and she thinks that the mathematics and philosophy departments in her university should look more deeply at the late eighteenth century once more, and at how logic was once so naturally put alongside theology – if only to see what questions such a re-coupling of thought might now spark. She thinks more and more often, these days, that the great schism that occurred between these worlds back then was wrong, or at least too hasty. She fears this separation is now as irrevocable as the methods of logic are convincing in their worth to science.

At times, as she works, she hears a subtle creak from upstairs, or the movement of a chair or a table. She takes these noises as an indication that Alois is having one of his increasingly irregular productive days, and this suggests to her that he is free of pain. He makes no call for food or tea. After many hours immersed in her new body of work, she feels a presence behind her. She chooses not to look, but she is sure it is Alois looking with pride or perhaps even some envy at the progress she is making, filling page after page with thoughts and observations and criticisms and areas ripe for lingering over or questioning with future students who will be fanned out before her in a timber-panelled lecture hall the like of which he knows he will not see again. The presence stays there for many minutes and, though she does not look to confirm it's actuality behind her, she still comes to the conclusion that this presence, when it is gone, she will greatly miss. She will miss its lonely erotic allure and she will miss the way the form of her thoughts, when she speaks to Alois, adapt to their content with the ease of a bird's wing in turbulence. She stops writing and puts her head into her hands. The presence behind her scurries upstairs and into the room where Alois has been sleeping deeply for the last half hour.

Catherine gets to her feet and takes a cup of water from a jug on the sill. She knuckles some tears from her eyes as she looks out the rear window at the rain easing off, lifting skyward. She recalls the rather drab day when she was thirteen and her mother and she left their home in the Irish midlands for London. She recalls how her uncle, Gilbert, drove with such nervous care along the narrow and hedge-encroached roads overflowing with puddles, assuring his sister-in-law and his niece, as they bumped along, that they could come back to the house 'any time' during the summers. The house was sold on by this uncle within the year, bringing to a close the personal debts owed by his youngest and recently passed brother, Moore. Gilbert sent his mother to an old and august nursing home in a neighbouring county, where, in her room, on Sunday nights especially, she dreamt of the sea and, in the distance, her one love standing in a boat, forever pulling aboard a net of improbable proportions. Into Carolan's once home then moved a hotelier, who in the following years built a glass conservatory off either flank, extended the gardens into some acreages of the farmland and sold off most of what remained. Then, during the war, the hotelier moved to coastal Massachusetts and sold the house and gardens to an opportunistic local farmer, Quinn, who was one of the children who had shared the country schoolhouse with Catherine years before – the same child who had one day incorrectly proffered, to a broad-shouldered priest called Wall, 'Galway' as the second-closest city to Dublin.

Catherine and her mother bade farewell to Gilbert at Dublin Port and took the dawn boat through the rain to Liverpool. Then, five trains to London later, they were met at St Pancras in the smoggy darkness of evening by Catherine's aunt, Patty, now long-wed to this violent no-good that her older sister had in vain warned her against. Patty invited them to stay at her home, but Elizabeth turned the offer down, opting instead for a room in a cramped Hoxton boarding house three streets from her ageing parents' abode, a tiny two-roomed cottage once built for labourers belonging to an expanding ironworks some hundred years before.

Soon, Catherine enrolled in the nearest grammar school. She was twelve by then and, for the first year in these strange and at times hostile surrounds, she returned to the timidity of her early childhood. At the age of thirteen, halfway through her second year in school, her mother took ill – an exceptional bout of nerves – and Catherine was moved to her aunt's tense and unhappy house on the northern outskirts of the city and into a more sedate grammar, where her teacher, a Mrs Rhodes, recently arrived from Peeblesshire in Scotland, was a person more amenable in temperament to Catherine. With this, the timidity into which Catherine had regressed for over a year suddenly fell away and she found herself raising her hand more often in class and making the sorts of observations and corrections she had once felt so comfortable making to Master Francis back in that small country schoolhouse four fields from her once family home. In a few months, she excelled again, her mind opening up exponentially and taking on with a profound ease new ideas and visualisations in physics, mathematics, the vocabulary and grammar of Latin and, on certain days, the haptic intelligence of technical drawing – these classes held in a frigid classroom filled with embarrassed adolescent boys – and then she was moved, at the age of fifteen, a whole school year ahead. All of this amounted to her receiving, on a fine summer's morning in her aunt's suburban kitchen, at the age of seventeen and two months, an offer of a scholarship to study mathematics and logic at St Hugh's College, where, on the morning of her arrival at the swan-topped iron gate, on a blowy day early in the following September, she was told of the college's, to her, attractive aim: *to make it possible for women of modest means to live and study in Oxford.*

Another creak comes from the floorboards above Catherine, but she does not bother to look. She places her well-worn clutch pencil down into the gutter of her green notebook, takes a sip of water and, looking at the tiny fragments settling in Brownian swirls to the bottom of her glass, she begins to absently recite:

As some fair female, unadorned and plain,
Secure to please while youth confirms her reign,
Slights every borrowed charm that dress supplies,
Nor shares with art the triumph of her eyes.

1.

It is a week later and Master Francis, having wished the children in his class a happy and healthy summer holiday, makes off on his bicycle towards the lake at the foot of the hill.

For most of the day, he has imagined the instant when his unwashed body will crash into the freezing lake water and then, as he re-emerges, the great gasping moments of surface tension snapping in rings around his head, shoulders, hips, and then all of this descending into circles of glittering ripples expanding outward from his body when he dives once more, like an otter, beneath.

As he cycles to the lake, he remembers the funeral, three days before, of the photographer, Austin. According to the hunched-over local man he stood next to for some time inside the main entrance of the church, it was 'a well-attended affair'. It was also one with an empty front pew and, after the Mass, no queue of people formed to offer their condolences, because there was no one to whom to offer them. There was a moment of muffled laughter and confusion as a queue tried to take form with nothing at its head. Master Francis learned from the young curate after the service that Austin had been ostracised by his family – 'turf farmers and thatchers all' – stemming from deep divisions brought about by his mercenary ways, imagined to their fullness during and immediately after the Civil War … 'A hand in the destruction of his brother,' was whispered …

No one at the head of the church knew quite what to do with the coffin itself, until four men from the local newspaper and two from the undertaker's emerged from the throng and took it upon themselves to carry the long and unadorned coffin down the main aisle and into the back of a flat cart harnessed to a blinkered brown gelding. The congregation gathered around the cart, chit-chatting and greeting each other amiably, and as Master Francis stood to one side of all of this, he realised that these waves of gentle talk around the horse-drawn hearse were designed to draw ranks and to keep the silence of the universe away from the body of their unknown brother for at least a few earthly moments more. Then, the hearse pulled away, with a *clip-clop*, out between the pointed pillars either side of the gate of the church, where the cart and horse then eased right and right again, up to the graveyard, a quarter-mile away, on a rutted snaking pathway, at the end of which soon appeared, to the left of the mound of earth at graveside, the priest, a young altar boy, two members from the golf club and these four newspaper men again, there to lift the casket from the hearse and then unhand it with lengths of red rope below.

Francis remembers, while they all gathered in that gentle hubbub at the front entrance of the church, seeing Clare among a small crowd of women arranged in a U to the other side of the horse and cart. She was dressed in black and Francis wondered if it at all troubled her the thought that she was the last person to dance with the photographer, Austin ... He wasn't wrong. She had spent the whole funeral Mass looking over her shoulder, trying to catch Francis's eye, if only to distract her from the thought and the growing feeling of guilt, soon put aside, that she might well have been the last person to dance with Austin, and, if so, then she felt a tinge of shame at how joyless an affair she had made it to be.

The lake shore is empty and Francis gleefully disrobes as a chill breeze rises, rattling the long stands of rushes to his right, which wobble down their stems making circular excitations on the water.

Four fields to the west, Moore Carolan places the receiver of his phone down, and with quivering hands he lights a cigarette. His broker in London has told him that his recent investment in the dollar has been wiped out. 'Unforeseeable strengthening of the pound and franc,' he said. 'A fit of arbitrary optimism ... There's hundreds like you.'

Moore stands, with his palm hovering above his wrinkling pate, while looking out over the back lawn and onto the glistening lake. Then he goes to the drinks cabinet in the sitting room and, from in among the dark bottles of sea-lilting sherries and brandies, he lifts out a dusty bottle of whiskey he was keeping over for a good Christmas. It was a gift from his brother on the occasion of his completing the purchase of this house, more than a decade ago. He goes to the toilet off the half-landing and from a cupboard he pulls a large jar of sleeping pills and, with both, he goes to an outhouse to the rear of this home and he proceeds unsuccessfully to end his days.

Three evenings later, he stirs in his bed. Elizabeth and the local doctor stand over him as his eyes widen into consciousness. The setting sun throws their shadows onto the warped purple rectangles of light illuminating the wall behind them. Carolan looks at these two figures suspiciously, his grey eyes passing over their forms, computing their shapes as if working out who these strange people are, and to this he eventually says, 'I must be still here, so.'

Elizabeth places a hand onto his brow as her eyes brim with tears. With a groan, Moore Carolan rolls over in the bed as his mind fills with memories of his recent and exorbitant loss of money. The doctor asks to take his pulse, but Carolan waves him away and for the rest of the day he lies there and thinks deeply about what he can do to put his financial affairs back in order. Then, some hours later, he composes in his head a letter to his brother, Gilbert, in which he delicately requests a loan that will give him a footing again at the bottom of a ladder he has already grown tired of ascending, but against this loan he knows that he will have to offer his portfolio of shares and the deeds of his house and farm.

2.

With a clutch of her red frock in her fist, Catherine chases along the path that arrows between the empty bungalows and the dunes. She's running away from Alois's house, in which he now lies unconscious, she believes, or perhaps even passed on. She runs and runs, gasping for breath, until she arrives at a broad junction in the road that leads on to the city of Aberdeen.

It begins to rain as she flags down the first car she sees and begs the driver, an aged ironworker from Fraserburgh, and whose accent she at first struggles to understand, to get word as quickly as he can to a 'Dr Bain on Don Street in the Old Town'. She asks the ironworker if he knows where Don Street is.

'Aye, ah ken,' he replies.

'Should I come with you?'

'Nae need, love,' and he speeds off.

Still painfully breathless, she runs back through the sea drizzle towards the house.

Meanwhile, in the upper-floor bedroom, Alois has woken. He falls from his bed, seeking water, but instead pulls himself to his feet and goes to his desk, where he clumsily lifts a box of matches and, putting six together, steps to his curtain and tries to light it up.

The curtain fails to light. Then he takes another six matches and, while watching them flare, he holds them to the curtain, from which now comes smoke and a small searing flame. He collapses back onto his bed as Catherine rushes indoors below.

She runs up to the bedroom, where she shrieks in a strange register of shock and happiness when she sees the flames climbing the flimsy brown curtain, all telling her that Alois is certainly at least still conscious.

Then, her face altering into a look of impassivity, she pauses and stares at the flame engulfing the base of the curtain and silently licking the wall. She considers for a moment stepping back and simply closing the door over, returning downstairs, gathering up her notebooks and clothes and leaving without ever looking back. But instead she steps forward and yanks the curtain from its railing and stamps on it till the flame dies to nothing. The room is still filling with smoke, so she creaks open the window and throws the singed and smoking curtain onto the path below. Then she goes to Alois's bedside and places her cheek over his lips to see if there is any sign of breath. She hears the dry old croak she has heard for almost eight days now and she wonders, What kind of chthonic surge of energy did Alois summon to set his curtain alight? She takes the matches from the floor and makes her way downstairs to fill a glass with water.

She returns and pours some of this water into Alois's clapped-out mouth; then she sits back, tear stains drying on her cheeks, and, taking his hand in hers, she looks to her watch. Ten past three. She reckons, if Dr Bain is not here by five, she'll have to take to the road again to send more word.

An hour and a half later, while standing at the bedroom window, and with a surge of relief, Catherine sees Dr Bain's black Morris Minor speeding up the narrow roadway between the bungalows and the dunes. Alois has come to and gone under three times since she put out his flaming curtain.

After Dr Bain leaves, soon after dusk, Catherine sits at Alois's desk and rests her head onto her arms.

Dr Bain has left her a steel syringe and a vial of morphine for the night, and the bleak palliative aspect of this upset her so much at first that she did not want this contraption.

But, as it turns out, there'll be no need for Catherine to use the morphine or the syringe, because, during the earliest hours of the morning, when the sea outside falls once more into utter calm, and while Catherine lightly dozes off on the chair at the bedside, Alois will open his eyes a moment and in the umbrage make out a form that he will take to be his mother, from long ago, seated beside his bed and whispering to him that he ought to go out now and follow the dark up through the forest growing out of the foothills of a peak, which he knows, near to his childhood home, and from this continue on to a narrower and far darker path that will lead him, upon loosening stone, arduously upward into a sweet-smelling if eternal undergrowth.

And, with this, Alois feels some last thing in his body rise.

I.

Master Francis emerges from the lake and, upon the grassy shoreside, lies on his back awhile. His skin dries incrementally in the sun – water drops seeming to travel back up his arms.

The two months of summer break stretch out before him. He thinks about the letter he will write to Clare Dargan, telling her that he has decided to go to Dublin for the summer to work on the building sites, with a view to earning extra money, before returning to his rented labourers' cottage five miles north of B_ for another year of teaching and saving, all for some vague 'future plans'.

As he dresses, he wonders if he will perhaps meet a girl in Dublin. And he wonders if it is Clare in whom he has lost interest, or is it women in general. He has no interest in men either, he reasons, so maybe all it will take is to meet another girl, one perhaps less broad of hip and less coarse in her movement.

He mounts his bicycle and makes off up Carolan's meadow and towards the warrens of roads that will lead him to the main road in the direction of B_, through which he'll freewheel before turning left at Hotel Gonne's and on up the

Bog Road towards his lodgings. He wonders, as he pedals through the grasses, might it be wisest or maybe most chivalrous to meet Clare with this letter, in case he meets no such girl less broad of hip and less coarse in her manner in Dublin?

The sun comes out as the road veers towards the domestic bogs, filled with scatterings of working women and children and men, and as the hedgerow clears to give views out over the flat lands, Francis thinks of a postcard he received from his aunt Cissy in Chicago some weeks before, telling him how hard she's finding the work and how lonely she finds life in the house in which she serves. The other side of this postcard depicted the enormous yet stately Pearson Hotel, along the roof line of which ran a row of what to Francis's eye looked like street lamps, and he wondered, when he saw this image – and wonders now, cycling along the winding *bóithrín* – what sorts of gentlemen stroll about up there on an evening of a warm Illinoisan day, smoking cigarettes, he imagines, of an exotic kind, these men all dressed in three-piece suits, each with a trouser pocket full of folded *greenbacks*, and furthermore, he wonders, what might these out-of-sight gentlemen be talking about with each other as the mysterious and vast roofscapes of Chicago rush down towards the rippling navy blues of Lake Michigan in the distance?

It occurs to Francis as he pedals past the boglands, now filled with carts and more locals squinting in the sun, that it is of the advanced conversations these gentlemen are having, while criss-crossing the lamplit boardwalk on the roof of the Pearson Hotel, that he is most curious to learn.

2.

Catherine steps from a blue double-decker omnibus as it stalls on the side of broad and chaotic Union Street, which spears up the middle of Aberdeen. She walks, in her long woollen coat, head down, through the sunlit footpaths and carriageways, past the looming granite towers of Marischal College to Don Street and on up the gusty road to Dr Bain's surgery ensconced on the ground floor of a two-storey terraced house, on the upper floor of which Bain and his young wife for some years now have happily resided.

Catherine rings the bell for the surgery and, upon entering, sees Bain, stepping from the door of his office; he looks at her eyes and immediately takes her in his arms. As she sobs, he begins to rub her back, his lips issuing a soothing, 'Shhhhh.'

'There, there, lass,' he says.

He leads her into his empty surgery and sits her down, and for a minute or so disappears, only to reappear with a cup of steaming black tea and a pill to settle her.

He asks her when Alois passed.

‘I don’t really know,’ she says, looking into her cup. ‘I woke to him cold and inert on the bed this morning, and I came immediately here to you.’

Then, picturing Alois alone in the house, she puts the white pill to her tongue and takes a sip from her tea.

‘I didn’t want to stay there all day, doctor, while waiting for you to come. I couldn’t bear the place going dark with just the two of us alone inside.’

‘Probably quite wise,’ says the doctor, lifting his leather case from beside his chair and slinging his dark tweed overcoat across his arm. ‘Come, dear, we’ll drive back out together.’

That night, after Catherine leaves Dr Bain’s surgery with a slip of paper in her hand upon which Bain has scribbled a note for the hostess of Grigor’s Guest House, four houses down the road, explaining Catherine’s urgent requirement for two nights of board, she remembers that, in the slow commotion of it all, she has left her two notebooks and her books and pages out in Alois’s house beside the sea. She resolves, before taking her trains in three days’ time to Edinburgh and on to Oxford, that she will call back to the house, in the hours of daylight, to pick up her belongings, take a walk along the shore once more and, for an hour at least, sit at the kitchen table and think about Alois and their first careful, intimate evenings together in the bomb shelter beneath Guy’s Hospital, then in their halls in Oxford, and then, at last, in his timber house. She remembers, before she topples into sleep, speaking with Dr Bain about Alois’s dying wish to burn the house down, but with him inside. To this Dr Bain replied, in a pragmatism that came to him naturally, hands on hips as he surveyed the fine and comfortable structure, 'Best not be too hasty, lass!'

Then, later, in one quiet and strange moment in the night, when Catherine wakes exhausted from a deep and untroubled sleep in her guest-house bed, she recalls something Alois said to her one afternoon a few weeks back while she worked on this series of lectures based on this work of Merleau-Ponty: that he, Alois, had always admired the way she could bend her understandings of one discipline into another. He said that he admired her impatience and her 'cavalier itchy-footedness'. He said that how she could see patterns across disciplines, 'from mathematical logic, to language, to psychology, now,' was something he always envied from afar. And then, before he returned to his room upstairs, he said across the kitchen to her, 'But you know it to be all a total waste of time, C., because in the end you will simply run out of people you can talk to or people who might even be willing to listen.'

For a few years after, she will remember what he said with a weakening fondness, until one day she'll realise that these words of his, far from marking out a kind of care for her, more so marked out for her an unasked-for set of limits. And, soon after this realisation, she will decide by year's end to leave St Hugh's and the medieval walls of Oxford for good.

1.

Moore Carolan lights a cigarette while listening to the workmen and agents drive off on the narrow road that winds west and away behind his house. These men are mid-harvest and, when Carolan ambled past at midday today astride Milly his mare, they told him, 'It's looking to be a bit of a thin year, sir.'

Elizabeth appears at the kitchen door and tells Moore that the editor of the local paper, Owens, dropped off 'a strange bit of post' at the house earlier in the day. She hands Moore the roll of drawings the deceased photographer Austin prepared for him.

Owens said to Elizabeth that they had found this roll of drawings on the table in Austin's apartment while they were clearing the place out, and he thought he ought at least to pass it along to the addressee.

Moore stubs out his cigarette, rises and takes from Elizabeth this strange roll of drawings. He makes to give Elizabeth a peck on the cheek, but she has turned away to return to the sitting room next door, to attend to Catherine and her homework. Elizabeth received word from Master Francis at the end of term to 'Please keep that brilliant young girl's mind at work through the summer!' Elizabeth sometimes looks on in wonder at how easily Catherine can manipulate enormous numbers around her otherwise smudgy copybook. It is as if by magic these crooked numbers – which Elizabeth herself is unable to check – appear on the page at the tip of Catherine's pencil. She has decided that, when Moore is back on his feet sufficiently, she will show him these developments and ask him to have them looked into. Until then, she aims to try to keep Catherine well occupied.

Moore, meanwhile, across the mahogany table in the dining room, is unfurling this roll of drawings. It soon becomes apparent to him that there are thirty-six drawings, eighteen of what look like golf holes and another eighteen of what look to him like topographical cross-sections of each hole from tee to green, showing lovely curves and dips for hills and swales. In the top right-hand corner of the last drawing, he looks over a general layout of these holes around a lake, the shape of which he recognises from the many Ordnance Survey maps he has seen before of the farmland that surrounds his home. He looks over these handsomely drafted designs for some fifteen minutes with a bemused expression forming across his face, all the while pulling each drawing over the next, until the phone in the hallway drings and he immediately steps away to answer, expecting news from his broker in London or, better still, his brother, Gilbert, in Guernsey.

Catherine, who has since stacked away in the adjoining sitting room the sheets of ruled workbooks and the sums books Master Francis gave her mother on the second-to-last day of term, ambles into the dining room and climbs upon the chair her father seconds ago vacated.

She pushes back one of these large rolls of paper and looks on for some time at this strange arrangement of curves and lines and words and numbers. Now standing on the chair, she takes in the numerals and letters, trying to discern some pattern, some meaning, but she can find no congruences between number or glyph. The whole thing is a plane of mystery. She clumsily tries another sheet, then another, but still she can make no sense or pattern out of what lies before her eyes, and yet, this aloofness, this difficulty, seems to draw her further in. She has the urge to find her oil crayons and, in between the swathes of lines, to colour in the whole picture before her, as if colouring such a thing will help her understand the picture better and, like a jigsaw, what hidden patterns it might bring forth.

Her father appears at the door, smiling. Gilbert, this rogue in Guernsey, has finally agreed to give him a hefty and face-saving loan under the conditions agreed about the deeds of the house and land.

He steps to the table and asks Catherine if all of this, as he gestures to the drawings, is of interest.

She nods enthusiastically.

And, because Moore is the sort who struggles to modulate his behaviour to others, he speaks to Catherine as if she were twenty years her senior and he describes how this golf course might fit and interconnect itself around the lake, which he points out to her through the dining-room window – this same lake in actuality glimmering in the distance and lapping quietly onto the ends of their bottom-most tillage fields. Catherine looks from the lake in the distance and back to the lake indicated in the centre of the small layout to which her father is pointing. Then, with his index finger indicating a large bold numeral at the top of each drawing, he tells her about how each 'hole' has a number and a shape and a character and a manner of approach and a scale of difficulty and length, and an orientation to the sun and to the prevailing winds, and in turn how each hole has an orientation relative to another and another and another. He shows her how the first hole leads to the second, the third, the fourth, and where the fifteenth criss-crosses three times with the fifth …

And, because Catherine has no knowledge of what golf is or most of the words her father utters, she merely assumes he is making all of these earthly observations solely about the numbers from one to eighteen. And, as his hands rove around these large diagrams of golf holes before him, there appear in a pocket of her mind curvatures that lead her into some deepening mystical if solipsistic sense as to what meaning these numbers, one to eighteen, might also carry and what properties they might possess. Then she visualises these numbers as individual objects of a kind with the numeral at the tip of a giant subsurface cone with patterns and clouds broiling, Jupiter-like, across its surface. Then, she thinks, what might be the myriad properties of the numbers greater than eighteen, and do numbers increase in subsurface riches as they increase in size, or are all numbers, no matter how large or small, equally distinct and complex in this way?

To this, and to many of these vast new possibilities, her eyes suddenly widen, and, with that, to her father's now relaxed and cheerful face, she turns and smiles.

Days later, she will return to these drawings on her own and pore over them once again, allowing her excitement to become more and more evolved, inventing as time goes by new functions with which to manipulate these riches – functions far beyond adding or multiplication ... She will do this long after these drawings cease to be of interest to her increasingly financially stretched father. She will store them, like a secret, in an upright roll behind the least-used dining-room curtain, alongside a long-forgotten bottle of lemonade, and then unfurl them before school each morning, as if she were learning that the land around the lake at the foot of her father's property contains beneath its surface a magical multitude of planetary forms and interplanetary functions. She will be entranced by these strange planes of possibility and how they deepen her appreciation of these numbers, especially those from one to eighteen, and how she can herself sport across these planes and curves of meaning, reconnecting them in countless different ways, producing different hues and climates that will in turn produce reconnections towards a developing sum of numbers far above, until the day, some morning well into her ninth year, when she reads in the newspaper about the existence of a game called 'golf'. She will see in the back pages of the *Irish Times* an aerial photograph of a golf course and, alongside these bird's-eye views of fairways and bunkers, she will inspect a list of names of players who qualified for the weekend rounds of the Midlands Open at Royal Mullingar, and she will think that all of these people listed, like her, must also share this deep and multivalent view of these eighteen numbers she had, up to then, thought so secret and so special, and with this somewhat prosaic discovery her enthusiasm for these once abstract and profound arrangements will wane. And the names Austin once ascribed to each hole – each number – will over time fall away too. The words 'The Elms' will for several years no longer sit so proximate for her to the number eighteen, as if it were some parallel linguistic property of it, pointing to some mystical terrain, dotted out in trees and organ-shaped indentations of sand … But, like any obsession first met and nurtured in childhood, Catherine will never truly forget them, and at times of great stress during the war, while working as a junior nurse in Guy's Hospital, and to help distract her and a bemused Alois from the bombings overhead, or at other times simply to help her concentrate on the patient's pulse she is counting, she will find herself, instead of using numbers to count each wrist-throbbing beat, using in their place the names of these holes she remembers from her childhood:

Lake View
The School Master's Burn
The Coasts of Lovely Longford
Pitch and Toss
The Shape of Leix
Turlough's Pass
The Hazels

The Distant Valleys of Clare
Devil's Dance
Forest View
Austin's Favourite
The Rushes
Carolan's Dip
Turn for Home
Quarry's-Eye View
The Ashes
Mother's Door
The Elms.

And she will list these eighteen entities over and over again, until the minute hand on her nurse's pocket watch reaches the two-minute mark, and from this she'll discern for how long the patient at hand will be among us. For the more dangerously stricken patients, she'll count these soothing words aloud, or at least loud enough for the fading heart and mind before her to register these lilting words all indicating mysterious places and unbuilt grounds once designed by a tall man who passed away upside-down in a canal ... and who was responsible for these terrains that all funnel inevitably down into eighteen fictional holes of four and a quarter inches in diameter, and into which an equally imaginary white sphere of gutta-percha will, from moment to unbidden moment, appear at the lip of the diameter before plummeting with an echoing *plop*.

2.

Catherine Carolan walks alone on the beach beyond *Haus Alois*. She brandishes the blue-and-white child's kite. Then, she stops a moment and sets her shoulder bag upon the sand, then down beside it she sits and begins to unravel some metres of the kite's length of red twine. The sun comes out behind a scudding cloud as the breeze once again picks up. She casts the kite into the air, but it merely falls three yards from her feet, edge side into the sand. She makes an effort to stand, but then, with a gust, the kite is lifted and swept in a series of broad esses up into the sky, the blue-and-white crepe paper between the struts flapping in and out. The kite's drab little tail and the red line of twine follow it skyward, too.

She feels the slim twine zip through her fingers as the kite suddenly lifts dozens of yards above the shore, onward and outward, haphazardly now above the frothing waves breaking and running landward. She releases the fifty yards of twine to its end and, holding the last inch of it between her forefinger and thumb, she feels in her fingers the translations of the shivering and shifting kite way above. Cupping a hand over her eyes, she squints at the kite and its movements in the sky. She imagines in the same currents of wind a far smaller kite appearing alongside her larger kite, but this smaller kite, this model, is being held by Alois, sitting here on the strand beside her, and she begins to describe to him the movements of her kite: 'Dive, dip, swerve, Alois; fall, spiral, shimmy, shiver, collapse, Alois; rise, soar, spin, shudder, float, Alois …' And she imagines, then, Alois describing back to her, in words of a similar kind, the movements of his tiny kite in the air beside hers, and there are moments, she imagines, when she and Alois both alight at the same time on the same word to describe how their two kites, similar in design if far different in scale, are behaving in these same contours of wind. She pictures for a while these moments when they both utter an identical word. Then she smiles at the thought of looking at Alois's tiny kite sharing the same currents as her kite, and realising – in the moment she looks over at his small model kite, so as to compare the word she used to describe the movement of her full-size kite – that, in that fleeting instance, he has already moved onto some other description of movement and she has missed that moment when their kites moved in a way that seemingly fell into consonance.

Then, she releases her fingertip from her thumb and the whole kite and tail swoops out to sea, the red twine sine-waving haplessly after the blue-and-white squares. Then, in the stronger currents further up, she sees one of the kite's crepe squares rupture, then another, and then the struts of the kite begin to fold and the whole thing plummets downward like a broken bird, where it tumbles into the rushing sea, but well out beyond the break line of the waves, where this cheap child's kite is then broken apart by the heaving water.

She looks to the hollow booming sea and the clock-like groynes spanning along the strand to her right. She closes her eyes and pictures the empty jerrycan sitting in the middle of the ground floor of Alois's house, with the floorboards and columns lined out with the gasoline, all awaiting a naked flame to drop. Then she opens her shoulder bag and peers in at the folded drawing of this ground floor, showing Alois's red lines of gasoline. She pushes this and her two notebooks and papers – and some of her sundry clothes, a candle, a mirror and toiletries – aside and she lifts instead for a moment the last two notebooks belonging to Alois. She has taken them in the hope that, when she returns to St Hugh's, she will be able to see if there was any merit in the thoughts he managed over the five weeks or so that he was in her care.

I.

Master Francis, with his belongings in a canvas rucksack strapped upon his back, cycles through the sunny warmth of midday. He is taking the narrow, hedge-lined road towards the butcher's in the village to the west of B_.

He paid up the last month of his keep at the labourers' cottage just north of B_ and told the owner, an aged local historian called Whelan with a lisp and a club foot, that he'd be back again in September to teach. Whelan waved him off saying he'd keep the place dry and warm for him, 'No bother at all, Master Francis!'

As he approaches Clare Dargan's village, Francis dismounts and walks the bicycle along the road. He has a letter for Clare in his trouser pocket, but he wants to straighten this letter out before delivery, and he doesn't want to enter the butcher's with a canvas sack on his back while perspiring so heavily. He wheels his bicycle around to the rear of the church at the top of the village. A young grey-haired priest emerges from the entrance to the sacristy. He and Francis exchange timid glances as Francis leans his bicycle and bag against the wall.

'Hello, Father. A nice morning we've had all in all,' says Francis, turning.

And to this the priest nods to Francis and saunters off.

Francis circumnavigates the church, clinging to the shade until the sweat on his back ceases to flow and begins instead to cool. As he walks, he thinks about how best to approach Clare with this news of his imminent summer-long departure.

He checks his watch, takes the letter from his pocket and makes off down the street towards the butcher's, out through the front door of which appears Clare, to smoke a cigarette. She lights her cigarette before jetting the smoke from her lips as she gazes up and down the quiet street. Then she spies Francis approaching. She smiles broadly and waves, before putting the cigarette out. She steps on the stub, in the way of her father, which Francis, as he goes, notices with a flicker of revulsion that only emboldens him further in his mission, for now at least, to cease proceedings.

He hands her the letter and speaks to her a moment, struggling to look her in the face. She pushes some ringlets of her fair hair off her brow. As he speaks, she smiles into the beginnings of a grimace that transforms into a lesser smile, then a frown, a nod, then an even weaker smile once more, but one where, above, her green eyes suddenly moisten. Francis halts a moment, then puts out his hand to shake hers, but at this strange show of formality she turns to go inside, and Francis does nothing to halt her; instead, leaning forward on his toes, he remains lingering outside the butcher's. Then, as the tinkling door claps shut, he turns and makes his way back up to the church, and without a moment's hesitation takes his bicycle from the rear wall, throws his sack over his shoulder and strikes out for the small informal country train stop, where the main train line heading east veers closest to the canal, at what they call locally the 'Lock Fifteen' stop.

On arriving in the city that evening, he'll pedal from Kingsbridge Station out to his aunt Monsie in the city-village of Sandymount, who – from the two diminutive twin sisters next door, the Ryles – will secure Francis lodgings for the summer, over most of which he will work on the other side of the River Liffey, on a building site for a newspaper office block called Independent House. And, on Fridays, after receiving pay from a slight foreman hailing from Kilkenny – Russell, a stonemason by trade – he will return back over the river by ferry and, from there, he will go out for a dance, and one evening near the end of July he will meet a dark-haired girl with the likeness of Mae Laurel, an actress he fell in love with when seeing her some weeks before in the cavernous Stella Cinema, she starring in a short pre-show film with the alluring title *Near Dublin*. He will tell this dark-haired girl, the evening after their first electrificating kiss, of her likeness to Mae Laurel, and she, with some wit, even a kind of hauteur, will take to calling him 'Stan'. The dark-haired girl's full name, he will learn, after four consecutive Friday nights together in this dance hall off Abbey Street, is Maura Joan Robinson, but she, some otherwise thrilling weeks later, will tell him, at the bottom of the steps of that same dance hall – the Mitre's Rose – that she has been proposed to by a south-side barrister, several years her senior, and she will recommend to Francis, on the steps of that dance hall, that he ought to 'away now and paddle his own canoe'. She'll leave him that night wholly dejected and, after another fortnight in this dreadful and filthy capital, growing more provincial and godforsaken by the minute, Master Francis will call it a day on the building site and say farewell to the two ancient and tiny Protestant twins, his caring aunt Monsie too, and he'll take the train back to the small country station, Lock Fifteen, and from there he will cycle with pace towards Clare Dargan's village in the smaller district to the west of B_, the tired late-summer fields spinning by – he remembering with relief the measured, ambiguous tone of his letter to her some months before – and when he arrives at this small village he will once more park his bicycle behind the church and let himself cool awhile before walking to the butcher's on the main street, but as he approaches the premises he will see outside of it a young man with a bicycle, idling, smoking, he the eldest son of the school headmaster, a lad Master Francis had taken to be a friend, and the young man will turn at the tinkle of the opening butcher's door and greet the radiant Clare with a nod and an offer of his crossbar, onto which she, smiling, will gracefully slide as this eldest son of the school headmaster pushes off, and they will wobble and then glide away down the street until the carriageway veers right, whereupon they will disappear behind the bend and towards the river bridge under which – as Master Francis well knows because he was told by Clare in urgent whispers on that night of dance some months before – lies a coveted spot for those who are young and falling in love, and to which Master Francis, had he stayed around, she would have gladly led.

2.

Catherine Carolan wakes from a nap as her train turns in a gentle rattle south-west at Stonehaven and on towards Dundee. Across from her sits a plump man reading in the flickering light *The Manchester Guardian*, which he rights, then rattles, then folds and, at a headline, peers. He re-adjusts his pince-nez on the bridge of what was once a badly broken nose, now congealed so incoherently together that the left-leaning septum almost wholly closes the nostril, and which at times and with a deep-winter head cold leads to this man emitting from his nose the faintest of whistles.

She decided to leave Aberdeen a day early, on account of the owners of Grigor's Guest House 'needing her room back' for the premature arrival of an unexpectedly large intake of theology students up from Cambridge, long booked in for a conference at the main university building in the Old Town, half a mile away. She was ready to leave anyway, or at least this is what she told them.

She gazes out the window now at the sea beyond the cliffs and on towards a headland, at the end of which turns a sturdy windmill, and she thinks back to the electricity-generating windmill her father had built to the rear of an outhouse. She remembers those loose lines drooping down to a generator that ran to their damp milking sheds in order to power a lone end-over-end milk churn – a mechanical armature fitted to the turning handle of the barrel, over and over with the odd clap, crackle and zap of the electricity amid the slosh of turning milk and the low growl of wood moving over wood. With these strange sounds from her last years in Ireland in mind – *The never failing brook, the busy mill, / The decent church that topped the neighbouring hill* – Catherine closes her eyes, knowing that any rest now would be prudent to take so as to best prepare her for the onward trip south overnight, where she expects to spend many hours sitting up and swaying uncomfortably on the stiff old second-class benches of the sleeper train rumbling out of Edinburgh, over the gentle border lands, into England and on towards what she has made as home in Oxford.

Some hours later, with a bump, and slowly raising her head from her knees, Catherine wakes, thirsty, from a deep slumber, just as her train pulls out of Leeds. Over the last few days, when she wakes from sleep like this, so collapsed is her psyche that in rush the clearest memories of her father from years ago, often just incidental images of him standing at a junction in the ground-floor corridor of their old farmhouse, always looking the other way, through a room and its tall sash window and onto the rolling land outside. This time, though, as she comes to on this rattling train, moving south and into the dark belly of England, she sees him leaning over a table in the sitting room, with the light pouring in from the twin gable windows at either side of the fireplace, and as his cigarette smoke spirals from his bent fingers, she sees beneath them a curl of paper and, with this, she recalls those large old numbered drawings showing golf holes interlinked around their lake-lined land. Her mind's eye, with glass-like clarity, roves over the surface of this sheet of paper titled *18, The Elms*, re-seeing the glyphs and marks and swerves – *Par 4, 415 yards, Stroke Index 3*. Then, leaving this sheet of paper behind, she imagines, for a moment, herself outside and travelling back to that house, down the tight and winding roads, past the forest and bracken hedges and on until she meets an opening at a turn, when the silage-scented land opens up and then descends down to the bright lake of home, where, one field over, stands the house, pale, its roof edging into the sky, its four walls filled now with the voices and the breath of strangers, themselves constructing memories of their home from what will become, at some painful juncture in the future, little but fleeting planes of darkness and light closing in and around the gentle glow of persons from there now gone.

I.

Master Francis spies amid the sun-gleaming trees at the base of the hill a line of three barefoot children approaching the schoolhouse. He steps closer to the front window and lights his third cigarette of the morning. The headmaster Foynes next door is noisily sweeping his room, having arrived back after the summer break foul-tempered and poorly prepared.

It occurred to Francis over what remained to him of the summer holidays that, aside from his usual teaching duties, he would take it in hand, for the years she would be under his tutelage, to educate Catherine Carolan on an advanced track of her own. He was curious to see how this fascinating young mind might grow and to what capacities, and he wondered what this advancement might look like, sound like, and how it would confound and perhaps amaze him day to day in this small schoolhouse room. Through August and early September, he spent several afternoons a week in the local library – Pierce Hall – researching second-level mathematics, some logic and second-level poetry. At times, when he looked up from his notebook, a thought would ghost him:

What if this is all for naught and she shows her capacities to be little more than 'above-average'? Then he'd push this thought aside and set to relearning other number systems and summing functions beyond those usually encountered in the senior years of primary school, all the while making notes and charting out a loose course of study for her, which over the evenings he would tighten and refine, drawing it out in coordinates of learning across a terrain whose extents followed the months of the school year.

Over the next four summers, such will be Catherine's voracious improvement that he will be forced to return to the local library to study mathematics more complicated than anything he ever encountered himself in secondary school or teacher-training college, and of which he sometimes feels it is beyond his ability to gain any realistic grasp. By the time Catherine turns ten, Francis will recommend she take lessons in applied mathematics from a retired army engineer, a Colonel Ramsay, living in an estate house to the east of B_ – who by then will have for some years run a company making and installing wind turbines for progressive farmers. It will be with him that Catherine's mathematical abilities will extend with ease into the realm of what the engineer refers often to as 'application', which, once she grasps the relationship between equation and model and coefficient and actuality, she won't so much bore of as sort of mentally wander off, in search of purer parts of this game where new pockets in her mind might be popped luxuriantly into being. This will become her addiction – that feeling of a moment of realisation. And she will become addicted over the years less so to its scale as to the texture of its originality.

One day, after all of these efforts, Francis will realise that he has exhausted the capacities he and this retired army engineer have to hand, to the point that he will consider but ultimately not pursue monthly trips for her to Dublin to speak to a famous professor of mathematics there by the name of Daddy Orr. This sense of exhaustion will strike him fully – like a minor note dinging in his chest – one bright afternoon late in the spring of 1929. Catherine will have just turned twelve and will have seen, not two weeks before, the limp figure of her father hovering above a shed of dark-eyed and thumping cattle, hanging from a roof rafter having lost all he possessed on a surge then a catastrophic collapse in the share value of American Steel. And on this day she returns to her classroom – and some minutes after she has completed an hour of 'modelling probabilities' with Francis, and following it up with a deeper study, now incorporating the other three eldest children in the class, of two stanzas from the middle of 'The Deserted Village', *Ill fares the land, to hastening ills a prey, / Where wealth accumulates, and men decay* – Francis, leaning over Catherine as her neighbour reads aloud, will see that she is no longer looking at her poem, but is busying herself instead with the careful circling of the elements of a set of equations she'd solved an hour before, and from each function in each equation on her page she will draw a line, at the end of which she will write the word *human*, and then from each circle around each number she will draw further single lines and at the end of each she will write the word *inhuman*. And when Francis sees this word *inhuman* dotted so obsessively around her page of otherwise clearly worked mathematics, he will step back silently from Catherine and return to the head of the class and engage them all in a conversation of the kind that will expand for the rest of the school year, crushing the untenable expanses of time previously given over to mathematics, in the hope that he might be able to offer Catherine at least something of what he has come to know and love most – poetry. And he hopes that he can do this for as much time as she is under his tutelage, which he with regret will believe, even then, might not be for nearly long enough to overturn the damage he has done.

Within a few months, Catherine and her recently widowed mother, Elizabeth, will leave for London and he will never see light of her again, until some decades later, while poking around, late in life, among the shelves of new books on the first floor of the august and bright Harold Washington Library, not two streets from his cramped studio apartment in central Chicago, when he will come upon a new book on linguistic philosophy – *A Short Treatise on Roofing* – one that has caused a minor stir in mainstream literature, written by an up-till-then unknown if long-passed Dr Josef Alois. It is a rather slim book only recently translated from German by a translator with the same name as the young girl he'd once struggled so manfully to educate. Francis will pick up the book, read a few lines on the cover and from a few pages within, and study some of the simple-seeming diagrams dotted through the sections. He will note from the title page of the book a brief dedication: *For Alois; translated out of a sense of duty and care. 'C.'* And from the colophon he will learn the name of the publisher, an obscure academic press in New Mexico, and he will see too that this Dr Catherine Carolan works, at the time of writing, at the University of Albuquerque. He will picture himself for a moment travelling by bus to Albuquerque to visit this very old student of his from that small country school back home, and then he will dismiss this thought as he places the book back down. And, with the bell for the library's closing ringing in his ears, he'll leave through the front door and on to the busy and spring-wet street, and he will then take the Blue Line way across town for his evening shift as a senior clerk in the timetabling offices of a local shipping conglomerate.

2.

On the first morning back in Catherine's halls of accommodation in St Hugh's, she wakes to the sight in her mind's eye of a Tyrolean-styled house, by the North Sea, engulfed in flames. She spends much of that morning in bed, until early afternoon, when she wanders down the sunlit but abandoned corridors to a wing of capacious technical-drafting rooms, just beyond the library, where she then slides from a broad cupboard seven large sheets of paper. The next day she spends in bed, taking only an evening meal, by which time her temperature has dropped from a feverish high to a sort of hot daze. Then, for the next seven days, she sits at her desk with these seven sheets of paper, and she drops her usual ordered and rational thoughts away from her mind and into the upper half of her body, as it were, suppressing the urge to work from top to bottom and from left to right, down and across the page. She sits there for hours on end, thinking in gesture, mark-making, single letters, glyphs, fragments of poetry, sometimes even turning the page over to pursue some piecemeal memory, thinking all the more deeply, as the hours and days then pass, while loops and scribbles and impulses appear upon each new sheet of paper, all the while keeping her cloudy subsurface planets of numbers at bay, until they begin to grind out in the background a music that comes to her mind through a kind of spontaneity and whim that grows into feelings of passion and a quickening of breath.

From all of this, she sits there and produces first one sheet and then another and another, all composed of markings that lead her into the realm of chance while facing her away, for a while at least, from logic or syntax or even the shadows of rationality. Until, on the last day of this activity, she becomes aware only of these shadows as the sun meets her back and their dark forms stretch along the ground from behind her, creeping out over her feet, as it were, to which she merely steps onward, awaiting their return until, at the fading of the likelihood of their return, she relents – relaxes, even – then becomes somewhat scared at the opening sublimity of these new feelings of thought, whereupon, with two last markings, she rolls up her seven sheets of paper and, with a growing sense of embarrassment, puts them all away.

In the following weeks, having fully recovered from this spell of *poor health*, she finalises in her green notebook her lectures for the coming term, and begins to compose a paper in her navy one on 'the probabilities of shapes in three-dimensional systems', a series of thoughts that will end a year later in a mathematical object that will become known as the Carolan Coefficient, but will end up being found only in the footnotes of the more hidden academic recesses of probability theory.

Then, almost two months later, on the night before her first day of teaching, she rolls out her seven large and, to her, mysterious drawings to see what on earth had been going through her *addled mind*. She enjoys what she sees: seven sheets with decreasing traces and marks indicating simple contours of thought, but with both sides of the sheets employed in all of these stagings, as if to suggest each contour holds not just a surface but a pulsating if invisible undersurface too.

By the middle of the decade, Catherine will finally tire of Oxford, its protocols, the weather, and she will pack up and leave forever, taking on instead a teaching post that becomes available far away in New Mexico, in what will soon become the University of Albuquerque. She will hear about this post from a colleague, Tinney, in Dublin, and a von Neumann in Princeton, with whom she'd corresponded for many years previously about 'random searches' and 'the probabilities of shapes on topological surfaces'. She will be enticed by the idea of New Mexico and the promise of wide skies and wider stretches of warm land.

On her last day in Oxford, she will take a walk first to the market off the high street, where she will purchase two nadorcotts for after evening meal. As she walks around the market, she will think of Alois and she will feel a sadness descend a moment. Then, on leaving the market, she will decide not to avoid, but instead to step wholly into this land of loneliness, and she decides to do so with the armour of her intellect as aide and standard bearer. Then, on her way back to St Hugh's, she will visit the meadows that stretch out beyond the playing fields of Christ Church, and she will try to picture at the end of this swaying meadow a row of deciduous trees leading to a broad and still lake with a bird of unknown breed lifting from its surface. Then, after dark, she will pack one suitcase before she takes her trip over land and sea and land, and she will decide, too, that she will wear open sandals in her new home. By way of books, she will merely bring Frege's *Conceptual Notation*, Alois's last two notebooks and her scroll of seven 'drawings'.

Every summer in Albuquerque, for the first half-decade or so, men in fine suits from trading companies in New York will visit her office and try to lure her to the city to bend her strange work in probability into the worlds of trading and actuary. They will offer her many of the comforts of the city and vast sums of money too, but she, with an inbuilt fear of large and sudden sums of money, will turn each of these advances down and happily return to her life as a college lecturer and tutor. She will talk to these men about the collection of 'dwarf palms' she cultivates and how she is working, these days, on the probabilities in the morphings of the leaves of each type.

Then, one day, during a summer semester in the early sixties, she will decide for safe keeping to have her seven large drawings framed, but in double-sided glass and in frames that have handles on either end, so each frame can be manipulated and easily turned over and back by any curious viewer, as opposed to these picture-like objects, say, hanging inertly on a wall. She will lean these drawings in a neat stack against a section of wall in her office, at the foot of a set of shelves holding books and plants, in the modern and bright staff-building of the University of Albuquerque. And, if a playful enough student asks about these strange things stacked upon her floor, she will take them out and speak at length about them in her strange multi-clause, but grammatically complete, sentences. Otherwise, if a student is seeing her about a specific problem in their coursework, towards which – notebook open – this student directs her attention, Catherine will lean towards this student and give her whole to the issue, the problem, at hand.

A senior lecturer in art history at the university will call often for a while. And he will look with admiration at the waves of Catherine's grey hair as she describes to him how these drawings came about. On his last visit, he will invite her out for dinner and Catherine will wonder to him aloud, 'Whatever for, Chuck?'

In quieter moments in her office, she will be most attracted to the seventh drawing of this set, and on very quiet days will pick it up and turn it about and note how one side contains in the centre of the upper third a single curved 'X', while on the other side, in the same position, will sit a curved '∧' – the logical notation for 'and' – these two marks being those she last inscribed on that final feverish afternoon in St Hugh's many years ago.

Then, one day, well into her sixty-fifth year, she will realise that the side of this sheet of paper containing the 'X' is a sky of sorts, holding a thought without collision, and that this thought, as it were, is being illustrated as being free to continue on its trajectory, while, on the other side of the sheet of paper, she will realise that it too is a mark in a sky of sorts, but this curved '∧' illustrates instead a thought that has been fully met, agreed upon, understood and brought in its essence to a halt.

'Both beautiful if ill-formed birds,' she'll say to herself, 'one preying on the other, but entirely in the wrong plane of desire and habit.'

That night, after she makes this observation and before she leaves her office for her apartment two streets north of the campus, she will, for a moment, be ghosted in the corner of her mind's eye by another possible world of thought – *Amidst thy desert walks the lapwing flies, / And tires their echoes with unvaried cries* – as vast to her as it will be vague. She will then see this parallel world not as the white squares to the chessboard's black, but as a plane of translucent and unconnected fragments above them all. And she will wonder if tomorrow she will wake with the daring required to step away from those black and white squares that have led her all of her life to here, and will she turn instead towards the translucent fragments and, unsure of her footing, step onto this untethered plane of thought at the threshold of which she will be made to meet once more the native brilliance in her bewilderment.

I.

A swallow swoops down by the schoolhouse window and up into a small hole beneath the gutter.

The line of three young children walking some moments before along the base of the hill in the distance now appears in a ragged loop from behind the hedging at the entrance gate to the school.

Master Francis steps back from the window as the sun returns outside and he goes to his table. He takes a deep draw from his cigarette and leans it into the ashtray; then, he pushes his books, sticks of chalk and his pencil across the surface of his desk and awaits the quiet rap on the classroom door.

Soon, with a knock and creak, the three country children will appear, and these children, each in turn, will approach him, smiling, to hand up their sods of turf.

But, because this is a warm and clement day, Master Francis will decide not to burn a fire in the classroom at all. Instead, he'll stack these dried-out sods of turf beside the hearth, storing them all for later in the term, when the weather out there turns cold, and the land less lively.

A note on Herr Doktor Josef Alois

The character of Herr Doktor Josef Alois is fictional. He appeared in my mind's eye while reading Wittgenstein's *On Certainty*. Alois is not intended as a historical fictionalisation of Ludwig Wittgenstein, despite some aspects of his thought and life stemming from some of Wittgenstein's thoughts and some happenings in his life.

A note on Catherine Carolan's navy notebook

The ideas on number theory and logic that appear in Catherine Carolan's navy notebook stem from Gottlob Frege's *Begriffschrift* (*Conceptual Notation*, 1879) and his *Die Grundlagen der Arithmetik* (*The Foundations of Arithmetic*, 1884). I have taken my understanding of Frege's discoveries and thoughts and reworded them in the way in which I think Carolan might express these ideas.

On page 52, the calculation 21 x 23 is shown using a version of the ancient 'Chinese stick method' of long multiplication.

REFERENCES

Beaney, Michael (ed.), *The Frege Reader*, Wiley Blackwell, 1997

Carter, Zachary D., *The Price of Peace: Money, Democracy, and the Life of John Maynard Keynes*, Random House, 2020

Goldsmith, Oliver, *The Poems and Plays of Oliver Goldsmith*, Griffith, Farran, Okeden & Welsh, 1886

Heidegger, Martin, *Poetry Language Thought*, translated by Albert Hofstadter, Harper & Row, 1971

Levi, Carlo, *Christ Stopped at Eboli*, translated by Frances Frenaye, Penguin Classics, 2000 (1947)

Merleau-Ponty, Maurice, *The World of Perception*, translated by Oliver Davis, Routledge Classics, 2008

Wittgenstein, Ludwig, *On Certainty*, translated by Denis Paul and G. E. M. Anscombe, Blackwell Publishing, 2008 (1969)

Wittgenstein, Ludwig, *Philosophical Investigations*, translated by G. E. M. Anscombe, P. M. S. Hacker and Joachim Schulte, Routledge, 2000 (1953)

Wittgenstein, Ludwig, *Tractatus Logico-Philosophicus*, translated by D. F. Pears and B. F. McGuinness, Routledge, 2009 (1922, translated by F. Ramsay and published by Kegan Paul, Trench and Trübner)

The Great Philosophers, BBC television programme (1987) – a conversation between Bryan Magee and John Searle
Men of Ideas, BBC television programme (1978) – conversations between Bryan Magee and A. J. Ayer, and Bryan Magee and Bernard Williams

ACKNOWLEDGEMENTS

Thank you as always to Niamh. Thank you also to Rowan Cope, Libby Marshall, Georgina Difford, Penelope Price, Rita Winter and all at Serpent's Tail for their thoughtful contributions. My thanks to Dr Thomas Raysmith for his valued help.

Very special thanks to Marianne Gunn O'Connor.

I'd like to also gratefully acknowledge the Arts Council of Ireland for their continued support of my work.

My thanks to Tuskar Rock Press, Profile Books and especially to Peter Straus.

And finally, my sincere thanks to Colm Tóibín, who edited this book.